LUST

THE DARK KINGS

CONTENT WARNINGS

Content Warnings: The Dark Kings is a high steam, high action dark romance series. The following content warnings should be considered before reading them: Dealing with previous trauma, assault, miscarriage, murder, sex trafficking, drug use, depression, anxiety, PTSD, bipolar disorder, gun violence, kidnapping, sexism, prostitution, elements of BDSM such as impact play and restraints, electro stimulation, knife play, primal play, CGL relationship, Shabari, profanity and sexually explicit scenes. This is a Why Choose romance. If you have any questions please reach out to the author directly at info@nikkirome.com.

To all my fellow kinksters and smut lovers. May these three men haunt your nights in all the best ways. If you can't have them in real life then you should be able to scream their names in the privacy of the late night reading hours. This one is for you.

Lust by Nikki Rome

Published by Rome Publishing Group

www.NikkiRome.com

© 2022 Nikki Rome

All rights reserved. No portion of this book may be reproduced in any form without

permission from the publisher, except as permitted by U.S. copyright law.

This book is a work of fiction. Names, characters, places, and incidents are products of

the author's imagination or are used fictionally. Any resemblance to actual people,

living or dead, events or locations is entirely coincidental.

For permissions contact:

Info@NikkiRome.com

Cover by Alt19 Creative

CONTENTS

Chapter One	1
Chapter Two	9
Chapter Three	19
Chapter Four	27
Chapter Five	35
Chapter Six	47
Chapter Seven	57
Chapter Eight	67
Chapter Nine	77
Chapter Ten	87
Chapter Eleven	97
Chapter Twelve	105
Chapter Thirteen	115
Chapter Fourteen	125

Chapter Fifteen	133
Chapter Sixteen	143
Chapter Seventeen	153
Chapter Eighteen	165
Chapter Nineteen	177
Chapter Twenty	191
Envy: A Dark Captive Mafia Romance	197
About the Author	199

CHAPTER ONE

VALENTINA

Gunshots never sound the same. I always found it strange how people would report hearing them when you can never tell for sure if that's what you are hearing. If you are the one shooting the gun, it sounds different from when someone else is. If you are standing close to the person being shot, is sounds different from watching someone get shot far away. The shots I hear now are close. Too close. I know they are close because they have that strange buzzing sound that guns with silencers have, a sound you don't normally hear unless it's right on top of you.

I moved the bed in the room I was being kept in. It wasn't my bedroom, but the place in our basement that he put me in when I didn't behave to his liking. I shoved it to the side of the cramped space and slid behind it. It wasn't the first time I tried to hide and it wouldn't be the last. I froze as my heart nearly exploded from my chest. There were heavy footsteps in the hallway and men yelling, but what I didn't hear was anyone at my door. At least not yet. I made myself even smaller and slid underneath the bed. I remember hiding from my father there as a young girl. It was stupid, really. He was the one who threw me in here, so he always knew where to find me. I didn't spend all of my childhood hiding under beds on a cold, damp concrete floor, but I spent more time here than I wished.

This time it had been six days. I knew it was because I keep track with the little stones I have collected over the years. No one suspects stones as anything to help me through my time here. The people sent in to feed or clean me just assumed they were part of the dirty floor. I pulled my legs into my chest and wrapped my arms around them. From where I was, six stones meant six days. One more day and I'd be taken from here and given to a man who disgusted me. The filthiest wise guy out there. Angelo Costa was a vile human being and at twenty-one years old, I'd be his sixth wife. If the rumors were true, then he killed at least half of the previous women he married. He was old enough to be my father and any time I'd beg or plead for it not to happen, my biological father wouldn't hear of it. I was nothing but a pawn in their fucking games, and I was sick of it.

Two more shots went off and could have sworn they were right outside my door. My father kept guards standing in the hallway. No one could get past them without killing them. I took slow, steady breaths that I had practiced over the years. My mouth got me thrown in here when my father and his latest wife sat me down to tell me I'd be leaving for the Costa Estate in seven days. The news made me sick. Death would be sweet compared to what I'd face there, but my so-called family didn't care. Why would they? My father's latest business aligned perfectly with what the Costa's did and the unity of the two families via our marriage would make them twice as large. Twice as likely to overthrow the real Kings of New York City.

I heard a scraping sound at the door and the hushed voice of a man.

"Hurry, we don't have much time."

"I know that. Now shut up so I can fucking concentrate."

They sounded familiar, but I couldn't place their voices. It's not surprising, there were so many people in and out of my life, it was impossible to keep them all straight.

"He'll kill us if we fuck this up."

"I know that, you fool. Now shut up."

I prayed they went past my door and the scraping noise I had heard was just my imagination. Silence was worse than the sound of the gunshots. They weren't my father's men, which meant the guards were dead. I opened my eyes and looked across the small room again. One, two, three, four, five, six. One, two, three, four...

Counting the rocks wasn't calming my nerves, nothing was.

"There, I got it. Stand back."

"You sure?"

"Yeah, I'm sure."

"Pull the lock off and open the door."

They were coming for me. It wasn't a dream or a nightmare. It wasn't my mind playing tricks on me, as it often did after days in isolation. There were two men outside my door and they were here for me. My breath was shaky, and I was losing feeling in my arms from clasping my legs so tightly. A fleeting thought of escape passed through my mind. Hiding here was pointless. No one would be dumb enough to believe my father would have a locked, guarded empty cell in the basement. Fighting seemed impossible, though. I was weak from the small amounts of food and water. Not to mention the complete lack of physical activity. The longer I was in here, the worse it got.

My body shook as I heard the metal lock fall to the ground. When the thick door opened, I couldn't help but look. Two sets of booted feet entered the room. Then, just as suddenly as they were there, one was dead. When the sound of the gun went off, my body jerked in response. A man fell to the ground as blood pooled around his mangled face. I couldn't pull my eyes away. If he were alive, he'd be looking right at me. Instead, I stared into the dark dead eyes of a dead man I didn't know. The amount of blood was massive and increasing by the second. My body rocked back and forth with the slightest movements while I tried my hardest to keep from screaming.

"Fucking shit," the other guy cursed as blood trickled toward his boots.

He stepped over the dead man and closer to the bed that was my only shelter. His large dirty hand reached right in front of my face as he grabbed the frame and pulled it from over the top of me.

"So much trouble for one little bitch," he spat out as he towered over me, "Come, get up. I'm running late."

I didn't move. I just curled my head to my legs and closed my eyes while praying to everything holy that this was just a psychotic break.

"I said, get up!"

The man leaned down and grabbed my arm. He yanked me to my feet as I screamed and kicked. Trying everything in my power to keep him away from me. I was no match for him. He was huge and smelled like a bottle of liquor and stale cigarettes. The smell alone made my stomach queasy as his arms came around me like a vice grip.

"You stupid bitch, just stay still."

I had no choice but to comply. The lack of air from his grasp made me dizzy. My body went slack, and he loosened his hold just enough for me to pull in a full breath of air. I wish I could say it was sweet, but it made me gag. He stunk like a dead man walking, and my situation was dire. I had no idea if my father and his men were even in the house. Maybe they were dead, maybe I was free. Freedom seemed a strange thought to have considering my current predicament, but being out from under the control of my father is one kind of freedom I thought I'd never have.

"Who are you?"

He just laughed.

"Listen, I don't know who sent you after me, but I am worth a lot of money. We could work together. Just tell me who sent you."

He laughed again, a throaty noise that caused him to cough in my ear. It was wet and made me want to puke, but when he kept coughing, he had no choice but to put me down. He sat me on the bed and pulled a gun from behind his back in one quick movement. If he wasn't nearly choking to death, it would have been impressive. He continued to cough up a lung as he threw a pair of cuffs at me.

"Put those on."

With the gun pointed at me, I didn't bother trying to fight it. I put the first one on just loose enough not to cut into my skin and for the second I used my thigh to close it, since it was clear my kidnapper couldn't be bothered. I sat on my bed as he pulled himself together. How the hell was this my life? Sitting here cuffing myself while some asshole had a gun pointed at my face? It wasn't the first time someone had a gun pointed at me, but that didn't make it any easier to remain calm. I rocked back and forth again, trying to relax, hoping the fool in front of me didn't accidentally set off the gun. It would surprise you at how often that happened. Men who thought they were big and tough pointing guns at others with no sense of gun safety. I learned to shoot before I learned to drive. Unless you plan to kill them, never point a gun at someone. Never take the safety off unless you plan to kill them. Never put your finger on the trigger in case you planned to kill them. My cousin Mario beat the rules into my brain again and again as he taught me. You wouldn't think it was so difficult, but now I sat there with a man pointing a gun at me that had no safety on with his hand on the trigger. Killing me meant he wouldn't get paid, so clearly, he was a fucking fool.

"I could help you. Did the Costas send you? If not, then I'm sure they will pay for my return."

"The Costas. Ha. All you stupid fucking families think you run everything around here. You have no idea how many times I've faced stupid men who think they rule the world." My eyes widened as he put his gun away and pulled a syringe from the pocket of his shirt.

My body tensed as he stepped forward. My fate was sealed. I lost this round. I closed my eyes, ready to take what was coming, when I felt the needle prick my neck. At the same time, the sound of another gun went off. This one was loud, even with the silencer. Small concrete boxes that pretended to be rooms created an awful echo. It wasn't the needle that made me jump, or the noise. It was the slick, wet liquid that seemed to have burst from the man in front of me. The needle was still sticking from my neck and my eyes were getting heavy. I dragged them upward and saw the splattering of blood that covered my white nightgown. I felt it on my face and tasted it on my lips. The man's body was now crumpled on the floor, nearly on top of the other man. Standing over them both was the last person I would have expected. My eyes closed as my body fell and all I could hear was a deep, arrogant, unapologetic voice.

"Ragazzina, I'm here for you."

CHAPTER TWO

DANTE

I'm not a fan of messes. As conceited as it sounds, I have people for jobs like this, but tonight it was different. Tonight we were coming for Valentina and I didn't trust anyone with her life but us.

"Fuck, Dante. What the hell happened? She's covered in blood."

"It couldn't be helped. Where's Nico?"

"Hunting."

"He doesn't have time for that."

"You tell him; he doesn't fucking listen to me when he's like this."

I watched as Ares, my best friend and second in command, stepped over the two dead men and reached for Valentina.

"Seriously Dante, did you have to shoot him so close to her?"

I didn't bother answering. Her body had fallen to the side when the drugs took hold of her system. If she wasn't covered in blood with a needle sticking out of her neck, she'd look like a sleeping angel.

"If Nico sees her like this, he's going to lose his shit," he continued while he removed the needle and laid it on the bed next to her. Then he stood and checked the dead man's pockets. "No key."

"It's fine. She'll be easier to transport if she's restrained."

"She's not a fucking prisoner."

"Are you sure?" I asked, waving my hands around the dirty little cell we found her in. Most of what we had planned wasn't even finished, but the first few steps were done. We had her. For the first time in years, I felt as if I could breathe easier, but we were so far from a happily ever after, it was fucking hilarious.

"Meet me out front. I'm going to find Nico."

I turned and made my way back upstairs. Everyone down here was dead. In fact, I would be surprised if I found anyone upstairs breathing. Well, anyone other than Nico. I followed the yelling that was traveling throughout the house. As I moved my way through, I passed multiple men who were bleeding out all over the white marble floors. It was a shame really; the blood would never come out of the smooth soft stone. I shook my head as I entered the kitchen. There I found Nico, covered in blood and swinging a meat cleaver repeatedly into something behind the counter. Given the amount of blood spray, I was certain it wasn't a chicken cutlet. He screamed like a monster every time he swung it in a downward direction, but was quiet as he pulled back up. I took that as my opening.

"Fratello, enough."

Nico stopped mid-swing and looked in my direction. With the cleaver held high above his head and the maniacal smile across his face, he looked like a demon walking the earth.

"Come on, we have her."

I didn't wait for him. There was no need. I heard the cleaver fall to the floor and the wet squeaking sound of his boots behind me as I made my way through the foyer and out the front door. It had been years since the three of us worked together like this. Sure, we worked together every day, but not like this. Wet work and kidnappings were things of the past for us. A warm feeling of nostalgia came over me as I descended the steps and crossed the driveway to our black Cadillac Escalade. I got in on the driver's side and glanced in the rear-view mirror. Ares held Valentina in his arms like a small child and was wiping the blood from her face as Nico approached. He reached for the door and went to get in before I put my hand out to stop him.

"Absolutely not."

"What?"

"You've covered in blood and brain matter. I'm not letting you in the car like that."

"What do you expect me to do?"

"I didn't expect you to beat a human to death with a meat cleaver."

"Well, I did. So now what?"

"Take your fucking clothes off."

"Here?"

"Yes, here. Bag them in the trunk."

"You have got to be kidding me."

"Can you two take this pissing match up later on? It's time for us to get out of here." Ares was getting impatient, but he was right.

I looked into my rear-view mirror and saw four white vans were heading down the long private drive.

"Just fucking do it so we can leave," I snapped at Nico, who was already removing his shirt in the driveway.

I pressed a button on the dash and the back hatch went up. It didn't take him long to strip out of his clothes. The four vans pulled into the circular drive behind us right as he was getting back into the car. If I wasn't so pissed off at him, I'd laugh. He sat in the front seat in nothing but a black pair of boxer briefs, boots, and blood. His face, hands and hair were still splattered, but at least he wouldn't ruin the upholstery. I put the car in drive and made my way back to the expressway as men and women in white Tyvek coveralls piled out of the vehicles and began unpacking everything they would need. I was heading to the villa. My family estate was where we were most comfortable. Tonight we could breathe deeply since the Romanos were no longer something we needed to handle. However, tomorrow, when Valentina didn't show up at the Costa Estate, there would be a whole other slew of shit we'd need to deal with.

"Any idea how long she'll be out?" I asked Ares, catching his eye in the mirror.

"No. I pocketed the syringe. I figured Dr. Anders can use it to find out what they gave her."

"I'm not calling him."

"What? Why not?"

"The fewer people who know where she is, the better."

"But what if she's hurt?"

"Is she?"

"How the fuck would I know? That's what we have a doctor for."

I shook my head and gripped the steering wheel a little tighter. Valentina wasn't with us for thirty minutes, and we were already arguing over her wellbeing. Taking her was nothing compared to what we were about to contend with. Ares could hate me for all he wanted. I wasn't calling in a doctor to handle a sedative. She'd wake up... eventually.

I pulled up through the guard gate at the front of our property and down the long driveway. The ride was quiet. Nico had turned in his seat and couldn't pull his eyes away from Valentina. Much in the same way, Ares was staring down at her. I couldn't blame them. The delicate features of her pale white skin and dark black hair made her appear like a porcelain doll. The first time I saw her, she was only sixteen. I was twenty-six at the time and my father made a deal with hers that she'd be mine. She looked like a baby to me back then, but her mischievous smile and gorgeous looks never left me. As she grew into her own, we would see her at events, fundraisers, and all the other bullshit our families had to do for the city to maintain the illusion of proper businessmen. When she walked into a room, every man wanted to be with her and every woman wanted to be her. Valentina Romano was a young girl who was the envy of everyone around her, and she was mine.

I stopped the car at the front entrance while three of our guards descended the steps in our direction. Nico got out but didn't make a move to go inside. Instead, he stood waiting for Ares to exit the vehicle, with Valentina in his arms. I walked through the front door and handed my keys to one of the men.

"Have it cleaned, and burn Nico's clothes. They are in a bag in the back."

I walked toward the hallway that contained our bedrooms. Our home was left to me when my father was murdered. My grandfather had constructed it when he first came to the states from Italy and it would remain in the Corsetti family for generations to come. Family and tradition were the two things that kept us going. Without them, we would be nothing. I had a room prepared for Valentina and that's where she would stay until I decided otherwise. After learning how she was treated in her family home, I knew the cells downstairs wouldn't be fair. There was a lot we needed her to learn before she would be allowed to roam our estate, and I wasn't planning on opening myself up to any issues before I was ready.

"Cut her free, bath her and change her clothes," I said to Ares while I avoided looking in their direction. It was too much to see her like this. I needed some time to get my head clear. It wasn't just that she was unconscious and restrained. She was too thin, and she looked as if they hadn't even allowed her to bathe regularly. The woman in Ares' arms was breath-taking, but she wasn't the Valentina we knew. Things had gotten worse for her than we realized and the guilt at leaving her there was eating away at me.

"Fine."

"Nico, come with me."

"No, I'm not leaving her."

"You'll come with me or you won't see her again."

"Fuck you. Why does Ares get to stay with her?"

"Because you're half-naked and covered in blood. Clean yourself the fuck up and meet me in the office. We have things that need to be taken care of now. Valentina can wait."

I watched as he turned, raised his fist and slammed it into the plaster covered wall. I shook my head at him with a look of disgust. "We talked about this. If you can't control yourself around her, then I will keep her from you until you do."

He cursed again, but turned and went toward his room. Ares had already made his way into Valentina's bathroom, and I could hear the water running as Nico's door slammed shut. I stood in the hallway, torn over what to do. I wanted to push Ares away and take care of my little girl, but I also wanted to make sure my best friend wasn't losing it. By the sounds coming from his room were a clear indication he was tearing the place apart. This was hard on all of us, but Ares and I both knew it would be the most difficult for Nico. Reining in the chaos wasn't something he did well. I left Ares and headed to my room. I changed my shirt since it was damp with blood splatter and then pulled out a couple of joints and a few pills for Nico.

When I got to his room, I didn't bother knocking. I walked in and saw the damage. He'd be pissed at himself later when he had to clean it all up. The wet bar in the corner was untouched, so I went to it and pulled a bottle of vodka from it. Normally I wouldn't encourage this level of drugs and drinking for Nico, but we needed him semi-functional and coming down off a killing like that was never easy for him. His anger was palpable on the best of days, and this evening he had unleashed the monster inside him.

"Here," I said as I pulled open the glass door of his shower and handed him two pills and the bottle, "I left a joint on the vanity. Calm yourself down and meet me when you're ready."

He said nothing. There wasn't much he could say. Even now, I could see the rage flowing through him. I may be known as the ruthless leader, but Nico was unhinged on the best of days. I went back into my room and prepped a sedative for him, just in case things got out of hand. When emotions run high between the three of us, you never know what could happen. I capped the needle and slid it into my pocket, then made my way to the office we shared and dumped the burner phone I had used for the night. Maintaining this city was a full-time job that didn't end just because we had planned to kidnap our little girl. I picked up my cell phone I had left at the house and it was riddled with notifications. There was a problem at the club. Text messages from the managers and missed calls from a dozen different people. Since Ares, Nico and I ran everything together, one of us was always available for our businesses. Tonight was an exception due to the nature of what we needed to do. I'm sure their phones looked the same as mine. People rarely called me directly, so that meant most of them already tried Nico and Ares.

I dialed the club first.

"Social, what do you need?" Gina, the club manager, answered on the first ring, which only made me more concerned because she rarely answered the main line.

"It's Dante."

"Shit, sorry. I didn't mean to bother you earlier, but I couldn't get through to Ares or Nico."

"What is it?"

"Some dickhead OD 'ed in the bathroom about an hour ago."

I grit my teeth in irritation. The nightclub was becoming more of a hassle than it was worth. "What did you do with him?"

"I had two of the guys close it for now, but we have to get him out of here. It's still early and business is picking up."

"I'll send over a crew. Did he have ID on him?"

"Yeah, some douchebag named Tyler Hamlin. Looks like some rich bitch kid from the Hamptons."

"Great, just what I need right now."

"I watched the tapes back and found his friends. Sent some of the girls over to keep them entertained. When someone asked another where he went, Mandy told them she saw him leaving with a girl. They were too drunk to care."

Gina had been a loyal employee for as long as I've known her. Her father worked for my family years ago and when she came back from college broke and addicted to Hell Dust, I offered her a job on the condition that she sober up through a treatment program. She did, and other than the occasional set back, she was the best manager we ever had. You couldn't exactly hire people and train them not to call the cops when people overdosed. It was a learned trait that we valued highly.

"Thanks. I'll get people out there to clean everything up soon."

"I appreciate it."

I hung up the phone and found Nico standing in the doorway.

"Better?"

"No."

"Sit. We have to go over a few things before you can see her."

CHAPTER THREE

ARES

I had laid Valentina down on the bed while I prepared a bath for her. For some, it would seem strange to bathe an unconscious woman, but it wasn't near as strange as some of the shit I've done in the past. I ran the water in the oversized tub we had installed for her and stripped out of everything but my boxer briefs. If she woke up, I didn't want to terrify her completely, but I also didn't want to get my suit ruined any more than it already was. The water was warm, and the tub was nearly filled, so I went back to get her and lay towels out on the bed for when we were done.

Her breathing was slow and steady as I carefully removed her thin white nightgown from her body. Holding her to me throughout the ride did nothing but cause my need for her to grow. Even while asleep, her nipples had puckered through the thin cloth while I wiped the blood from her face. For that reason alone, it did not surprise me to find her without a bra. I couldn't help myself as I ran my hand down her chest and over both of her tight nipples that even now seemed to call for my mouth. The desperate desire to suck them and provide her with pleasure was difficult to ignore. Somnophilia was one kink of mine that she would need to agree to first. Her consent was the only thing that kept me from doing more than just pleasuring her breasts. I slide the small scrap of fabric that covered her mound from her body and threw both it and the blood covered nightie into the trash. Then, careful as ever, I lifted her to me and made my way back into the bathroom.

She was like my little doll that I treasured more than any other toy I owned. Her white skin contrasted with my tan, tattoo-covered body in the most alluring way. I descended the steps into the tub with her in my arms and lowered her into the water. Whatever the asshole had given her was still in full effect because other than goosebumps that covered her skin, there was no physical sign she knew what was going on. I held her in my lap with one arm under her neck as I let the water warm her body. After a few minutes, I reached for soap and began cleaning the blood and dirt from her. When I had first gotten my hands on the blueprints of the Romano Estate, I assumed the cell in the basement was for business, similar to our own. However, with more digging, bribes, and pay offs, I learned that room had a different purpose. It was where they would keep her when she stepped out of line, which seemed to be often if my intel was correct. Nico went into a week-long, rage filled bender when he found out and it had caused us to move up the plans we had to extract her. Anton Tirelli was a good friend who was in a shit situation with the woman he loved. Some assholes were trying to sell her off at the Romano's auction and resolving the whole mess took longer than Nico would have liked. Longer than any of us would have liked. When it was settled, we made our move.

Once I was certain Valentina was clean, I got her out of the bath and placed her on the white towels I had laid out. I slipped out of my wet boxers and wrapped a towel around my waist, then worked to dry her the best I could. Her long thick hair would take too long to dry properly, so I left a towel beneath her head as I dressed her. Dante thought I was crazy when I ordered everything I thought she may need. But now, as I pulled a pair of black silk panties up her legs, I was happy with the choices I made. I followed with a pair of soft leggings and a black hoodie for fear she would be cold and disoriented when she woke up. The last thing I wanted was for her to be suspicious about the skimpy nighties I had ordered. Once she was tucked into bed, I stepped back and gazed down at her.

"La mia piccola bambola." My little doll, I thought as I leaned over and placed a gentle kiss on her crimson soft lips. My cock was so hard it was painful. I needed this woman more than I needed to breathe. Of all the people responsible for bathing her, it was me. I knew it would be the second I saw her. Dante couldn't even look at her, and Nico was currently insane. It had to be me, but it didn't make things any easier.

I stepped back before I made mistakes I couldn't erase and left her room, locking the door behind me. I made my way to my own bathroom, turning the shower on as hot as I could get it. Sure, I was clean from the bath with

Valentina but I needed relief and didn't want to deal with a mess. I dropped the towel and stepped inside with my hard cock already in my hand. The hot water cascaded down my back and I leaned forward on the cool tiles. It brought a strange sense of reality to me as I closed my eyes and pictured my beautiful little doll.

Her dark hair against her pale skin as I held her still body in my arms was a fantasy come true. It was only topped by undressing her and holding her again in the warm water while I bathed her. I grasped my dick hard and moved at a punishing speed as I remembered the feeling of her curved ass up against my cock while I had her in my lap. Her silky skin was soft as I ran soap over her breasts and between her legs, leaving nothing to the imagination. I let my mind wander as my breathing increased and my heart raced. I imagined doing it all again, but without a washcloth between my hand and her skin. Instead, my roughened fingers would delve into her soft center, swirling inside of her, forcing an orgasm from her with nothing more than my fingers.

The images were too much to hold on to. I choked out a muffled groan as I bit my forearm, that held me up against the wall of the shower. The hot water did nothing to soothe me as every muscle in my body tensed and everything I held tight exploded all at once. My legs threatened to give out, but I locked my knees as the movements of my hand slowed, my breathing steadied itself and my mind cleared for the first time since I saw her.

La mia piccola bambola. She will be the death of me, maybe even the death of us all.

By the time I made it to the office, Nico was trashed, and Dante was pacing. Not a surprising scene in the slightest.

"She's bathed and in bed. In case anyone cares."

"What the fuck is that supposed to mean?" Nico snapped.

"It means, while you've been sitting in here getting wasted, I made sure she was taken care of."

"Fuck you." Nico went to stand, but Dante's voice caught his attention before he escalated. Something I was thankful for at the current moment.

"Sit down, Nico. Ares, another smart fucking remark like that, and I'll let him loose on you. Fighting amongst ourselves isn't going to help a thing."

I watched as he crossed the oversized office and sat behind the desk that once belonged to his father. The only things that changed about the office since we took over was that the sitting area was removed and two identical dark wood desks were added. One for me and one for Nico. Mine was riddled with computer equipment I used daily. Nico's workspace comprised a pile of dusty papers and a laptop that I'm certain he'd forgotten the password for.

"Sorry, you're right. The good news is, she seems to be in fine health. Too thin, but otherwise no bruises or scars. At least none given to her by anyone else."

"What does that mean?"

"She has small thin scars along both her wrists, and more on the insides of her thighs."

"Are you saying she harms herself?"

"I'm saying she has in the past. There are no open wounds, but we don't know how long he's had her in isolation."

Nico pushed himself up in a fury, knocking his chair over in the process. He looked like a bull in a china shop as he made his way out of the office. The only thing stopping him short was Dante standing between him and the open door.

"I told you to sit."

"Why can't I see her?" he screamed at Dante, spit flying out of his mouth as he spoke. His fists were clenched and his shoulders tense. Anyone who saw him like this would be terrified, but all it did was break my heart. Nico was the baby of the group, the youngest by only two years, but when we were kids, he was the light-hearted, funny one. Then, after Italy, he was never the same. No one could reach him, not even Dante or me. There were walls of anguish that held him together now.

I stood and walked over to them, placing my hand on his shoulder. "Maybe he could lie with her, just for a bit. I'll stay there with them. It will be fine. I won't let anything happen to her."

Dante's features of stone softened for only a second. It was so subtle if I hadn't been looking, I wouldn't have noticed. He turned his back on both of us and threw his hand up as he walked out of the office. "Fine. An hour and that's it. After that, I want you both out of there, or I'll drag you out by your fucking dicks."

Nico's entire body shook with relief under my grasp. "Come. I'll bring you to her."

When we got back to Valentina, she hadn't moved a muscle. Her dark hair fanned out over the white towel I had laid under her head and the blankets still covered her body. She looked peaceful, almost happy, if that were even possible to see on the face of an unconscious woman.

"What did you put on her?" Nico asked as he stood at the end of the bed.

"Some clothes to keep her warm. Her hair is thick and it will take a long time to dry. I didn't want her to get cold."

I watched as he walked to the side of the bed, lifted the white embroidered duvet and slid under it. Without a second thought, he reached for Valentina and pulled her tightly to his chest. I turned out the lights and took a seat in the corner. Nico held her as if she were the most precious thing he had ever laid his hands on. Her head was tilted into his chest, and I watched as he ran his fingers along her face and through her hair. I'm sure he hated me watching such an intimate moment, but Dante wouldn't let him near her otherwise. Although we had known for years Valentina belonged to all of us, she still didn't have a clue what her future would really look like. As a child, they promised her to Dante, but it wasn't just him, it was never just him. Allowing me to bathe her, or Nico to have this moment with her were all risks. She could wake up at any moment and lose her shit on us, but they were risks we were willing to take. Until Dante got his head out of his ass, and battled the guilt inside of him, we were all she had. The only question left was would she accept us for who we were, or fight us all for a freedom she would never have again?

CHAPTER FOUR

NICO

Rage is a strange feeling. It consumes a person at the best and worst times of their lives. For me, it started when I was younger. The inability to calm myself turned me into the monster I'm known as today. It never bothered me. I don't give a fuck what people around me think. But tonight was the start of something new, something different between Dante, Ares and myself. My rage was no longer the thing that held me together. Now the only thing that mattered was the dark-haired beauty lying in my arms. For the last three years, every decision we made we did with her in mind. When she turned eighteen and they did not give her to Dante as promised, our worlds fell apart. When you spend so long looking forward to something, you begin to think it will solve all your problems. Then if that thing is kept from you, or taken away, you have nothing left but the shit that surrounds you.

When I walked into Dante's office and he told me I had to change for her, I wanted to scream. It's not like I haven't tried to change. I have. I just can't control the monster inside of me. Over the years, they have diagnosed me with more acronyms than you would imagine. Massive depressive disorder, oppositional defiant disorder, post-traumatic stress disorder, bipolar disorder… the list goes on. There was a period where Ares and Dante did nothing but help me hunt down solutions, and at the end of it all, I turned into a comatose freak on enough pills to kill a small elephant. So I stopped. I stopped taking all of it.

I had no idea how long we had been laying there. The drugs and alcohol I'd consumed to calm down combined with her warm body up against me left me in a state of bliss I had never experienced before. Ares was still sitting there watching me. Dante didn't understand that I could never hurt Valentina. It would kill me if I did, yet he still didn't trust me with her. A soft sigh broke the silence and her hand that was caught between us twitched. Ares jumped up and came to the side of the bed.

"Get up, give her some space."

"No." I wasn't letting go. After what she had been through tonight, she didn't deserve to wake up alone, terrified, in a strange place. I ran my hand down her back softly as she moved carefully in my arms. I placed a kiss on her forehead ever so gently, but it was enough to wake her. Her body tensed and her eyes shot open. She pushed against me and yelled, but I held her tight, refusing to let go as Ares flipped on the light.

"It's okay, la mia bella ragazza. I've got you." My beautiful girl, I have you forever. My mind raced as she tried to pull herself from me.

"Let me go!" she grunted as she tried to knee me in the balls. The fierceness she displayed wasn't to be rivaled with. To survive as long as she had in that house, she had to be strong, but those days were over and now she would break for us. I grabbed her wrists and pushed her down onto the bed, covering her body with mine. I did nothing to hide how hard I was, but instead I pressed my hips into her. Her movements stopped, and she froze in place at the realization of what was happening between us.

"Stop fighting, little one," I said as I shifted my grip on her, holding her hands above her head with one of mine. I took the other and turned her chin so she was facing me. Tears had pooled in her eyes, yet I could see the defiance within her refusing to let them loose. "Your fight is over. We have you now."

Her body relaxed under me, and her eyes darted in Ares' direction. She still couldn't move her head, but when she saw him, she seemed to understand what was happening.

"Where's Dante?"

"Not here," Ares answered.

"Why? He said he came for me. Why am I in bed with you instead?" she said, turning back to me.

"You'll have a lot of questions that need to be answered, but first we need to see to your wellbeing. I'm going to ask Nico to let you go, but you will not run. Do you understand?"

It took her a second to respond, but when she did, it was with only a nod of her head.

"That won't work, la mia piccola bambola. You will answer with your words when we ask you a question. Let's try again. You will not run when he lets go, do you understand?"

"Yes."

I didn't want to let her go. I wanted to lean down and suck on her neck until I marked her. I wanted to tear her clothes from her body and fill her with my cum until she begged for me to stop, but with Ares there, none of that could happen. So I slowly loosened my grip and moved my upper body while still pinning her hips in place. That she left her arms right where I had her, spoke wonders of how well she'd submit in the future. She had no idea how much that thought increased my need for her.

"So beautiful," I heard Ares murmur next to me.

I moved off of her and Ares pointed to the bathroom. "You can freshen up in there."

She got up slowly, not ready to trust her body completely. Ares walked close behind her to make sure she was steady on her feet. As Valentina went to close the door, she turned back and took one last look at me. Her head tilted to the side and her mouth parted slightly. "Who changed my clothes?"

"I did, after I bathed you."

"You bathed me?"

"Yes."

"How long have I been here?"

"Only a couple of hours."

The expression that crossed her face was unreadable. It would have horrified most girls at the thought that a man stripped her down, bathed her and changed her clothes, but Valentina didn't seem to mind. At least she didn't show that she did. Maybe she was just as fucked up as the rest of us after all. The door closed behind her and I looked over at Ares. A look of trepidation crossed his face.

"You need to leave now."

"No."

"Nico, she needs to get acclimated to this new life slowly and we've already fucked up by allowing her to wake up like this."

"Like what? Lying with me? If this is going to work, then you and Dante need to fuck off. Whatever happens between me and Valentina has nothing to do with the two of you."

"You think that's the case? You're such a damn idiot sometimes. Brother or not, if you lose control and hurt her, Dante will put a bullet through your head."

"Let him fucking try." I got up and crowed Ares. We were nearly the same height, but I packed on a lot more muscle than him and he knew it.

"Don't make this so difficult. Just go."

"I'm not fucking leaving her!" I yelled as the rage that simmered just below the surface threatened to explode, "She's mine."

"She's ours. She can't know everything in one night. Give her time. We all need time."

"We don't have fucking time. Tomorrow, all this shit is going to unfold and we are going to war. Not a battle, a long ass war. That will be the next set of excuses. Nico go kill this guy. Nico go kill that guy. I'm not a fucking machine that you two can turn on anyone you want dead. The time it takes me to do all that shit would be time away from her, and it's not happening."

I was growing more and more angry by the minute. Fucking Ares, always thinking he knows what's best for everyone. The damn peace keeper of the group who did nothing more than piss me off. My fists tightened as I stood staring at his smug face and I lifted my arm before I had even considered the consequences. He ducked, and I hit the wall, cursing at the pain that radiated up my arm. I had thought for sure I bruised something earlier and now I knew something was broken.

I turned on him and fucking bellowed. The scream that ripped through me was nothing but anger and pain. If I walked out of this room right now, I didn't know when they would let me see her again. I couldn't change who I was overnight and the thought of losing her again after I just had time to hold her was too much. I lunged at Ares and caught him right in the middle, pulling him down into a heap on the floor. When most people fight it's chaos, the mind races and it's impossible to think straight, but for me, it was the opposite. Time seemed to slow down and with every punch he attempted, I could see it moving in my direction and avoided it. I flipped us over and shoved my forearm into his throat until he stopped moving.

"This is your fault! You did this to me!" I screamed into his face while he just sat there with a stupid fucking smile. Then I felt it, the prick of a needle that would certainly change the course of the night. I let go of Ares and rolled onto my back, staring up at Dante, who stood with an empty syringe in his hand.

"I told you he couldn't handle this tonight," he said to Ares while I slowly drifted.

"I know, but he deserved a chance to try."

"Where is she?"

"In there. She was asking about you."

"Help me get him up, then go see to her."

"She's going to want you."

"Not tonight."

I closed my eyes. The sedative he hit me with wasn't one that knocked me out completely. It just made me so exhausted I could barely move. Both of them helped me to my feet and nearly dragged me off to my room. They dumped me on my bed, but before they turned to leave, Dante looked back.

"I'm sorry, brother."

I rolled my head to the side, unable to look at him. I couldn't look at any of them. If this is what the future would look like, then I was in for a shitty fucking life. I didn't go too far tonight. I wanted to, but I controlled myself and neither of them knew how hard that was. Now it was the middle of the night. She was finally awake, and I wanted her. I wanted to be with her and instead I could barely hold on to consciousness. I closed my eyes, giving up on today. Fuck all of them. Tomorrow hell would rain down on us and then they would come to me, then they'd need me and maybe if I'm lucky she'll realize she needs me too.

CHAPTER FIVE

VALENTINA

The fighting in the other room did nothing to help me calm down. I had too many questions to think clearly, so instead I stood in the mirror and looked at my reflection. Recalling the few things I knew for a fact.

I was with The Dark Kings.

I woke up in bed with Nico Marchesi holding me as if his life depended on it.

Ares was watching.

Dante was nowhere to be found.

Now I'm standing in a bathroom, which it appears I've been in before... naked... with Ares, and I had no idea what to do with myself. The physical pull to Nico was unmistakable, but the look in Ares' eyes made me want to go to him. I hadn't been alone with them for more than a few minutes, and my mind was a scrambled mess. I was there for Dante, wasn't I? I splashed water over my face and grabbed a towel.

Nico sounded pissed at something Ares had said. Then there was a crash and a scream. Before I knew it, I heard Dante's voice. I wanted to open the door, to go to him and demand answers, but something held me back. He was the man I was promised to, and he had finally come for me. After all these years, he did what he had promised to do, but then he left me in the arms of another man. What did that mean? If he found out I was attracted to the others, would he send me back? I wasn't even certain it was really an attraction. Both of them were remarkably handsome. I knew them from social events, but never had more than a casual conversation with either of them. The problem was deep inside, I knew what pulled me to them was more than physical. It was like my broken soul saw something in them it needed.

I heard Dante talking to Ares. Nico was strangely quiet as he told him he wouldn't see me tonight. Disappointment invaded my brain and ran through me, causing a pain in my chest. He didn't want to see me. He didn't want me. I sat on the floor in the corner trying to piece together what had happened. I heard some shuffling around and then nothing. It was eerily quiet on the other side of the door, but I didn't move to see what had happened. Everything I knew about the Kings was that they were inseparable. Three men to be treated as one and yet here I was in their home, listening to them fall apart at the seams.

It couldn't have been more than a few minutes when I heard a soft knock on the door.

"Valentina, can I come in?"

I didn't bother answering. It was more of a formality than anything else. These men did whatever they wanted and although I should be terrified, I found it didn't bother me in the slightest.

Ares crossed the oversized bathroom and came to where I was curled up in the corner. He got down on one knee and placed a hand on my shoulder.

"I'm sorry you had to hear all that. It's okay now, you can come out."

"Where am I?"

"I think you know the answer to that."

"The Corsetti Estate?"

"Yes."

"Why am I here?"

"You know the answer to that too," he said, standing and reaching a hand down to help me up, "Come on."

I was hesitant at first, but then he did something that surprised me more than anything else that had happened that night. He reached into his pocket and lowered his hand to show me what he had. The palm of his hand was tattooed with a large star, but in the center were my six little stones from my room. I reached for them immediately and tears sprung to my eyes.

"You brought them."

"I did."

"Why?"

"The way they were lined up made me think they must have been important to you."

I clutched them in my fist and went to stand. "Thank you."

Ares was likely the most beautiful man I had ever seen. His strong features, beautiful tattoos and shoulder length hair gave him the look of a rocker god. I knew he owned a tattoo studio and when I was younger, I would fantasize about going there and having the one and only Ares Sabino tattoo me for the first time. Now here I was, standing next to the man, knowing that he had already seen me naked and my body flushed in response. I could feel the heat in my cheeks and he picked up the change between us. He looked down at me with a small knowing smirk and I couldn't hold eye contact any longer. My blush had overcome me and I looked away only for him to let out a little laugh that warmed my insides.

"Come, la mia piccola bambola, I brought up something for you to snack on while we talk."

He reached for my hand, and the electricity that ran through him into me made me jump. A jolt of lust and craving and everything you'd imagine if you touched a man that looked like Ares. I had never been with a man, but that didn't mean I didn't understand physical attraction. Ares was a walking sex god and being so close to him was harder than I thought. We made our way back into the bedroom and he helped me up onto the bed. I noticed a tray was there that I hadn't seen before and he pushed it to the side and sat in front of me.

"Water first." he said handing me a bottle. "We don't know what they gave you to knock you out, but it may take a day or so for you to feel like yourself again. Water will help."

"How don't you know? I thought you were the ones who took me."

"We did. But we only took you from the others who thought they could claim what was ours."

"Ours?"

Ares didn't answer, but reached for a strawberry and held it up to my lips. "Eat."

I went to reach for it but he shook his head and pressed it to my lips. "Eat."

I opened my mouth slowly, and he placed it gently on my tongue. The sweet taste of the fruit, along with the look on his face, made me moan in pleasure. My eyes had closed and suddenly embarrassment came over me.

"I'm sorry... I... I think I was just hungry," I said, trying to cover the erotic noise that escaped me.

"You are hungry. I can see that. But it's not for fruit, is it?"

Ares looked at me as if he could see the inner workings of my mind. Hiding from him seemed useless, but I'd try anyway.

"Maybe just thirsty then." I reached for the bottle of water and lifted it to my lips to take a drink. When I finished, he sat there with a ripe blueberry between his fingers.

"Eat," he commanded, and I opened my mouth. This time when I closed my lips around the berry, I realized my mistake. Ares hadn't pulled away, instead his middle finger, the one tattooed with a crown, was still there. I moved the berry to the side of my mouth and, without thinking, closed my lips over it, sucking as if it were the sweetest thing I had ever tasted.

"Oh, cazzo, Valentina. You're going to be the death of me," he said as he pulled his finger from my mouth and leaned forward, replacing it with his tongue.

Ares gripped the back of my head, holding me to him as his tongue darted in and out, swirling inside of me. My arms reached for him and pulled his weight onto me as I leaned back. I was dazed with need and I didn't give a shit. I wanted this, needed it. Ares was the one who would give it to me. His hand reached up under my hoodie and the feel of his coarse hands over my soft skin gave me the chills. My hips pressed forward into him, and I could feel his length hardening between us. When his fingers reached my small breasts, they wasted no time. He pushed my shirt up and his head moved until his mouth covered my nipple, sucking it so hard I could feel things twinge deep in my core.

"Fuck, Ares. Please. I need... I need this. Make me come," I begged, as if I had any idea what I was doing.

His hand traveled further south and slid into my leggings with little resistance. I opened myself for him and ever so softly, his large oversized fingers found the tight little nub between my folds. When he touched me there, my body shook with need.

"Tell me Valentina, are you a good little doll?"

"Yes. Yes, I am," I answered as his movements grew quicker and my climax grew in strength.

"Is my good little doll going to come all over my fingers, then? Will she do that for me?"

"Yes."

My need was insatiable. I couldn't hold myself back any longer and I sure as hell didn't want to. I had no idea what was happening between Ares and myself. It was as if I were someone else completely. That I had been basically kidnapped only hours earlier and now I was in bed begging for a man I barely knew to make me come was not lost on me. I ignored all the warning signs and pushed away the concern I had for my sanity as I let myself ride the wild wave of passion that was Ares Sabino. There would be time to question my judgement later.

"I can't wait. I'm going to come. More Ares, please," I begged, as he continued. Then he leaned over me again and bit down hard onto my breast, causing the tidal wave of pleasure to crash into me. I screamed out my release, unable to contain myself as he peppered my body with soft kisses until I caught my breath and pushed his hands away from my oversensitive clit.

Ares laid next to me and I looked over to him. He had his middle finger in his mouth and was sucking my juices from his skin. When he finished, he leaned forward and kissed me hard and needy so I could taste myself on his lips.

"So sweet," he whispered. Then, as if nothing had happened, he reached over and picked up another strawberry and slipped it between my lips.

"Will Dante be mad?" I asked after a few minutes.

"Dante is always mad."

"I mean about this... about what we just did," I said in between the bites of fruit and cheese that he continued to feed me.

"He may be mad that I tasted you first, but he won't be mad about what happened."

"I don't understand."

"I know, it's okay."

He didn't offer any further explanation, so I left it alone for now. I was sixteen years old when I first learned Dante would be my husband. My father's wife at the time explained to me what my duties would be, and I had no reason to believe that wasn't the case now. I saved myself for him, but now I was lying in bed with one of his best friends. After waking up in the arms of the other. Nothing made any sense right now, but I didn't want to press it. At the end of the day, I was still a guest in the home of the Corsetti Family. Men known to others as both protectors and killers.

"Who was trying to take me?"

"Tomorrow you were supposed to be sent to the Costas. You know that, right?"

"Yes. Was it them?"

"No. Another family hired the men who came for you. They had planned to hold you for ransom from the Costas in hopes they would pay."

"That's ridiculous. There is no way they would pay for me. That wretched old man would just let them kill me and find another wife."

"I know."

"So that's why you came?"

"It's part of it."

"Dante was supposed to come for me on my eighteenth birthday."

"I know."

"He didn't. None of you did. Why now?"

"That's a story Dante will need to tell you. For tonight, just know that you are safe and you will be taken care of while you are here."

"Are you sending me somewhere else?"

"No. You are ours. You will never be without one of us again."

Something about that made me warm inside. I had never been with anyone who claimed they would keep me safe. My father hired most people around me only to care for me, but they had no loyalty to me. The tone of Ares' voice made me believe he was telling me the truth. That as long as I was alive, I would always have one of them by my side.

"What happened to Nico?"

"He's... tired."

"Please don't lie to me. My whole life has been spent with people lying to me."

Ares leaned back on the pillow and looked up at the ceiling. He was quiet for a while and I held my breath, hoping he would tell me the truth. I lifted his arm that was next to me and snuggled into his side. He was warm and the overwhelming feeling of safety was something I could grow addicted to.

"Nico has some issues he's working through, Valentina. He struggles with things that are easy for most people and sometimes those struggles get the best of him. Tonight, you needed to feel comfortable, and we feared he would frighten you. Dante asked him to leave and he wouldn't. So... we made him."

"How exactly did you make someone like Nico leave?"

"A light sedative, nothing like what they gave you. Just something to take the edge off for him. Once he gets a good night's sleep, he will be better in the morning. I'll let him come see you then."

I sat up and looked down at him. "You drugged him? Like they did to me?"

"No, nothing like that."

"But it's the same, isn't it? You wanted him to do what you said and he wouldn't, so you knocked him out."

"Valentina, it's not like that. He knows what happens when he gets out of control."

"The man I woke up with was not out of control. In fact, he displayed more control over himself than you did just a few minutes ago. Where is he?"

I jumped down from the bed and crossed the room to the bedroom door.

"Where do you think you're going?"

"Away from you, that's for sure. Where is Nico? I want to see him."

"I told you he's asleep. He'll be up in the morning."

"That's not good enough." I yanked open the door to the bedroom, and it surprised me to find it wasn't locked. Ares let out a curse under his breath, which made it clear he hadn't meant for that to happen.

I stepped into the hallway and turned to the right. There were huge vaulted ceilings and artwork on the walls worth more than my life, but I didn't stop to admire any of it.

"Nico!" I yelled, as if he could answer me. I opened a couple of doors to find what appeared to be a half bath and a sitting room. Then the next door I pulled open was another enormous master suite, like the one they kept me in. I stepped inside and immediately smelled Ares cologne that I had been loving while laying with him. I looked around quickly and found it was definitely his living space. There was dark black bedding and huge art pieces that resembled some of the most amazing tattoo work I had ever seen in my life. If I wasn't so pissed off, I would have loved to spend more time in here, but I had a driving need to make sure Nico was okay.

I turned and pushed past Ares and back out into the hallway. As I went to open the next door, I almost succeeded until his voice stopped me.

The deep timbre and sheer aggravation that dripped from each word stopped me in my tracks. "What the fuck is going on here?"

I took one look at him and realized he wasn't talking to me. He wasn't even looking at me. I moved down the hallway, which unfortunately brought me closer to him, but it couldn't be helped.

"She's looking for Nico."

"Why?"

"She thinks we killed him."

I turned and shot Ares a dirty look before turning the handle of the next room. Finally, I found him. Laying in the middle of an oversized dark oak bed was the gentle sleeping giant. A soft snore echoed throughout the room as I approached him and crawled up into the bed next to him. I don't know what drove me to such insanity, but I needed to see him. I needed to feel him and know that he was okay. I reached my hand out to the side of his face and whispered my apologies. It wasn't his fault things happened the way they did tonight. It was mine. I had only just gotten here, and I was coming between three men who had spent their entire lives together. I placed a kiss on his forehead and then settled in next to him as Ares and Dante entered the room.

"If you want me to leave him, then you can just kill me now."

"Well, it appears our little one is quite protective of our brother, Dante."

"She is now. We'll see how long it lasts," he said, turning on his heels and leaving me alone with Nico and Ares.

I didn't bother looking up, but just spoke to him from my place in bed. "You can join us or you can leave. I won't have you babysitting Nico like he's a small child. He won't hurt me."

"You don't know that. You don't know him, or any of us, for that matter."

"I know what my heart tells me and this man would die before he'd hurt me. I could see it in his eyes."

CHAPTER SIX

DANTE

It was nearly noon and not one of the assholes I lived with made their way into the main house yet. I was normally the first one up and the last one to sleep, but Ares and Nico were taking sleeping in to a whole new level. Yesterday was stressful for all of us and last night was even harder. I had imagined Valentina would fight us, refuse to stay, and make a scene. What I hadn't expected was for her to push anything Ares or I said about Nico to the side and crawl into bed with him. Seeing her with him both hurt and healed something deep inside me. I wanted her to myself last night. I wanted her under me, but I wasn't ready yet. Seeing her here in our home after finding her the way we did made everything too real. The guilt of leaving her in such a shitty situation for so many years was eating away at me.

The plan was for her to stay locked away in her room until she agreed willingly to stay. But after last night, I don't think her leaving was something we had to worry about. That didn't sit well with me. I needed to know why, and I was getting impatient. They had slept long enough. I made my way back to the bedrooms and opened Nico's door. There, lying in bed, were both Valentina and Ares. Fucking hell, that's not what I expected either. Jealousy sparked its ugly head and surprised me. We had shared women before, but seeing them with Valentina without me felt uncomfortable. She let out a soft sigh and I watched as her arms wrapped tighter around Nico's center before I had enough. I banged loudly on the door three times and laughed as I watched them all jump.

"Come on, the day is nearly over and we have shit to do," I said, continuing to enjoy their angry state. As Ares threw a pillow, I dodged it and saw the most adorable expression I had ever seen on Valentina's face. Nico cursed as I walked to the side of the bed and reached over him for her. I slid my hands under her arms and pulled her from the bed as if she were a small child.

"They have had you long enough. You are coming with me."

I walked from the room holding the most valuable thing in my entire world. I didn't want to like it as much as I did, but having her in my arms was making it difficult to tamp down the feelings swirling through me. Lust was all it was. It was all it was ever supposed to be. She would be my queen, the woman behind the men who ran the city, but I never planned for her to mean anything more than that to me.

"Where are you taking me?" she grumbled as she rubbed the sleep from her eyes.

When we reached the double doors of my master suite, I stepped inside and crossed the room to the bath. I placed her on her feet and closed the door behind me, instructing her to take care of whatever she needed and meet me back in my room. I needed sometime alone with her, time to understand what she was thinking, without the influence of the others.

She didn't take long and came right to me. I had her take a seat on the small couch in front of the fireplace and she tucked her legs under her in the most delicate way.

"Is there coffee in this place?"

"Yes, I'll have some brought up for you with breakfast."

Standing so close to her, having her here in my room, were fantasies of mine for so many years. Even looking at her, I couldn't believe she was there.

"Why now?" she asked, looking up at me.

"It was time."

"But they told me you'd come when I was eighteen. That was three years ago."

"There were complications after my father died."

"What kind of complications?"

"Promises were made and never kept."

"So you just left me there. Which brings me back to my first question. Why now?"

"Did you not want me to come?"

"I wanted you to come when I was younger. I wanted someone to come and take me from that place. They had prepared me to be your wife, even though I barely knew you. I knew what was required of me and I gave into it years ago, only to be let down when you decided you didn't want me anymore. Do you have any idea how hard it was to see you over the years and then be taken back to that place they kept me? To see you with other women knowing it could have been me, but I wasn't good enough?"

I knew I should have said something to make her feel better. I needed to tell her she was wrong, and that wasn't what happened, but my anger was clouding my judgement. She had been fed so many lies over the years. I was desperate to learn all of them. There was more information I needed. I needed to know why she hated her home so much and what really happened there.

"What was it like living there? You call it 'that place' and 'the place they kept me' rather than home. You refer to your father as a stranger and yet I should be the stranger to you."

She turned her eyes from mine and focused on pulling apart a throw pillow that was sitting next to her. I didn't move; I didn't breathe. I just stood and watched as she worked through what she wanted to share with me.

"It wasn't always terrible. I love my father even after everything he's done. I mean, he's my dad and the only person I've ever really had. My mother died when I was born, you probably already know that, but other than my cousin Mario, I don't have anyone else."

I cringed at the thought that her love for him would come between us, given what we did last night.

"Tell me about when it was terrible."

"It doesn't really matter anymore. You aren't sending me back there, are you?"

"There is no place to send you back to. The home you once knew was destroyed."

"What?"

"It's gone, Valentina. The house was cleaned and burned to the ground last night."

"My father?"

I ignored her question. Now wasn't the time. "What did he do to you to make you hate your childhood home?"

"You saw where he kept me. I wasn't always locked in there. Most of the time, I was allowed in my room or the main parts of the house. I could even go out on the grounds sometimes with a guard. He always told me it was for my own good. That I needed to learn to behave like a lady for you and follow rules. He would tell me if I couldn't keep my mouth shut, and learn respect, then you'd never come for me. Or if you did, you'd kill me for stepping out of line."

"And you believed that?"

"I did for a long time. Then I attended a family wedding, and you were there. Do you remember? It was my cousin Maria's wedding."

"I do."

"I watched you that night. You looked at me in a way that made me feel special. I saw how close you were with Nico and Ares and I couldn't imagine you being so ruthless that you would kill a woman you were supposed to marry. I asked my father's wife at the time and she called me naïve. She told me I was a fool to believe The Dark Kings wouldn't kill me for disrespecting them."

"Did you believe her?"

"Maybe. I guess so. Our lives are different from most people. Growing up with the families we had, the expectations were different. I never went to a real school or out to the mall with friends. I didn't have sleepovers or a boyfriend growing up. Anytime I asked why, or questioned his plans for me, he would have me removed and put back in my cell. So eventually I just stopped asking."

"But you were there last night."

"I was. It was the sixth night."

"Why?"

"He told me Angelo Costa was coming for me."

"You didn't want Angelo? Even after I never came for you?"

"No. I guess I still hoped you would come one day. But if I married Angelo, that would never happen."

There was a knock at the door and I opened it, allowing the staff from the kitchen to come in and set up breakfast for her. She reached for the coffee as soon as they left, but wouldn't look at me directly. I couldn't tell if she was afraid of me or if she regretted what she had shared.

"Valentina, I want to set a few things straight," I said as I took a seat at the small table she had sat at to eat. "Ares, Nico, and I are ruthless men. We have done horrible things in the name of protecting what is ours and we would do it all again. I was young but not a child when my father planned for our marriage. I knew the second I saw you that you would be mine, and I never doubted that, not once. The month you turned eighteen, my father was killed. I had a lot of responsibilities that I needed to focus on but that didn't mean I wasn't coming for you. The arrangement between our fathers was part of a much larger agreement and when you came of age, your father hid you from me rather than turning you over. It was the first of many infringements I would uncover."

"But I was there. I was always at that damn house. You could have come anytime, but you didn't." I could sense her irritation.

"You said it yourself, our lives are different from most people's. It's not like I could just knock on the door and tell him I wanted you. It took time to ensure you were really there and put together a plan to make things right again. My father kept journals of his business dealings and as I worked my way through them, I learned the history between our two families was extensive. I had many meetings with your father trying to negotiate new terms and, in the end, force was the only way to ensure the promises that were made would be kept."

"So now what? I mean, I don't think I understand everything that is going on here. What will my father say when he finds out I'm with you? What about Angelo? Will he come for me here?"

"No one will come for you here, Ragazzina. You are safe from others under our protection."

I watched as she picked up her coffee and took a careful sip. She looked like a small child with her hair up and in the clothes Ares had dressed her, but behind those eyes was a smart and calculating woman. She spent a majority of her life preparing for this moment and now that it had come, I needed to make sure it's what she really wanted. I wouldn't stand for a weak and pitiful woman with no thoughts of her own. Valentina would need to show us who she really is before I'd be willing to accept anything from her.

"Today you will stay in your room. I have business to take care of with Nico, so Ares will stay at the house with you."

"I can't leave my room?"

"No, not yet."

"So this is what it will be like, then? The same as it was before?"

"It will be nothing as it was before. This is your new life, Valentina, but before I open myself and my family to the risks of keeping you, you will need to decide that you want to stay."

"I want to stay. I don't want to go back."

"I already told you, there is no going back. Your house and the life you knew there is gone. It's over and it won't be the only thing you will lose. If you chose to stay, you will become one of us. The Romano name will no longer be yours. You will become a Corsetti, and with it, you will hold the responsibilities our name carries. You will fall in love with us all, and that will confuse you. We do not hide who we are. We will not hide ourselves from you. You get the good with the evil, but it's a choice I will allow you to make."

"And if I choose to leave, you will let me?"

"I will."

She sat there contemplating her next question carefully. I watched as she tilted her head slightly and gazed up at me. She failed at hiding the slight smile when she asked, "Who are you talking about when you say us?"

"You already know the answer to that question."

Valentina grew quiet. There wasn't much more to say right now. I respected that she asked nothing further. The rumors about the three of us and our relationships ran wild. I'm certain she knew what she was getting into. Her silence spoke wonders. Valentina Romano wasn't just some poor little girl that had been locked away for years. She was a queen in her own rights, and manipulation was her best skill for survival. I stood and went to her. As I lifted her chin, I leaned down and placed a gentle kiss on her lips.

"Fino a tardi, ragazzina. I will be back later this afternoon."

She looked like an angel when I pulled back. Her eyes were still closed and her lips were slightly parted. I wanted to ravage her in the best ways possible, but after learning she had never even dated before, it only confirmed my suspicions that she was a virgin. I needed to meet with Ares and Nico. We had to adjust our plans with her based on this new information. I wouldn't hurt her, but I also wouldn't deny myself what I had wanted and needed for so long.

I left my bedroom to find Nico stumbling out of his room and making his way to the kitchen.

"Morning sunshine."

"Fuck off."

"Where's Ares?"

"No idea. He left when you came in like an asshole and ruined the best moments of my life."

"The best moments were while you were asleep?"

"Lay with her tonight and you'll know what I mean." He looked behind me toward the closed door of my master. "Where is she?"

"Having breakfast in my room."

He went to turn, but I stopped him. "Not now. We have work to do. Angelo Costa is publicly mourning the death of his fiancée."

CHAPTER SEVEN

ARES

"This is a load of fucking shit." Nico interrupted the silence of the office as he busted through angry and annoyed.

"Hello to you too."

"Angelo Costa needs to die."

"Although I would normally agree with you, it won't solve anything this time." Dante said as he followed behind Nico.

"How did it go?"

"As you would have expected."

He and Nico had left hours ago to handle the shit storm at the club and an issue with our supply chain. We had a recent drug shipment that went missing, and I largely suspected the Costas had something to do with it. While they were gone, I planned to spend the afternoon worshiping our little doll, but the second I opened my laptop, I knew that wouldn't happen. The news of the Romanos was spreading like wildfire, causing more problems than we had expected.

"How is she?"

"She's fine and in her room, with the door locked this time," I said as I pointed to the security feed on one of my monitors.

"Have you seen her?"

"Not much. The Costas have been stirring up shit everywhere and I've been handling rumors while you two were out gallivanting around town."

Nico let out an aggravated growl as he sat at his desk and pushed a bunch of papers out of the way.

"What have you heard?" Dante asked, taking his seat.

"Nothing we didn't expect. They sent men out to the Romano's property and met with the police chief. It's a good thing we pay well because he called me when they left and told me what he wanted. Angelo claimed his engagement to Valentina offered him the rights to know what happened, but the chief shut him down."

"Seems strange he would go the legal route."

"It wasn't all legal. While he was meeting with the cops, his men were scouring the property. It was probably all a distraction tactic. After that, they headed back to their church making a big show of grieving the loss of his dear friend and fiancée."

"Where are they now?"

"Waiting to hear from us. Angelo has requested a meeting."

Nico pushed back from his desk and paced over to the window. "Fuck him. That disgusting piece of shit isn't worth our time."

"Maybe not, but we still need to get a handle on the trafficking business he was in with Romano. It would be stupid of us to believe he'd just let the whole thing go with the other man dead."

"When is the next auction?"

I turned to Dante to see him tapping his fingers on his desk in annoyance. "Two weeks from now."

"We'll need to keep her here until it's over. I don't want Valentina caught between us and them."

"She asked about her father this morning."

"What did you tell her?"

"Nothing."

"She didn't press it?"

"No, but sometimes it's like I can see into her mind. Like she's tucking away bits of information."

"The woman survived years of abuse at the hands of a man who was supposed to nurture her. There is a lot to her we haven't uncovered yet. She's keeping details to herself right now, learning and trying to determine her place with us and within our business."

"Then let's show her," Nico said without looking at either of us, "That was the plan, wasn't it?"

"She's a virgin."

My cock immediately swelled at that bit of information. We had always suspected that would be the case, but to have it confirmed just ratcheted my need for her to a whole other level. Knowing that we would be her first and her last was the best thing I had heard all day.

"How does that change things?"

"Nico, the neanderthal... that's what I'm going to call you." The comment earned me a shitty look as he tightened his fists, ready to come after me.

"Don't think I already forgot how you two stuck me with a damn needle last night."

"Couldn't be helped," Dante said as he opened his laptop.

"Fuck off."

"How long are we going to wait?"

"It will happen tonight. I'll take her, but I want you both there. She needs to understand how things will work between the four of us. As for her learning more about our business, I want to wait. She mentioned her cousin to me last night and I don't know if she will try to get in touch with him. I can't risk a leak with everything going on. This morning I told her to take today to determine if she wanted to stay. If she doesn't, I will let her go."

"No fucking way. After all this, after all these years, you're going to just let her walk away from us?" Nico advanced on Dante, but he didn't even bother to look away from his computer. Sure, he was the big and scary Dante Corsetti, Don of the Corsetti Family and literal ruler over New York City, but he was still the guy we grew up with. He was the one who was devastated to learn his cousins Luca and Micah wouldn't stay and work with him. He was the one we made a pact with when that happened and at sixteen years old, we promised to never turn on each other. That was the only reason Nico was still alive after so many years of pushing him.

"She has a choice, Nico. I won't hold her against her will after what her father did. She spent her whole life locked up like an animal. You can't tell me that's what you want for her future."

Nico took a step back. He was pissed, but he couldn't really argue that point. When I finally landed an informant close to the Romanos, we were all upset over the intel that came through about Valentina. None of us had imagined how bad it was for her there. Why would we? As far as we knew, she had been taken to Italy and was being tutored there by private teachers. When Dante's father died, it was easy to believe she was better off without us. Those first few years were a mess, with so many enemies trying to rise up. By the time everything settled and I could focus on locating her, time had flown by and things were only getting worse for her.

"Did she say anything to you about it?" Nico asked.

"No, I didn't bother asking what her and Dante talked about this morning and she didn't share. I don't think she realizes yet that there aren't any secrets between us."

"Why do you say that?"

"Because she asked me again what you would think when you learned what happened between us yesterday. She wanted to know if you'd make her leave when you found out."

"What did you say?"

"I told her you wouldn't, but that you'd be pissed I got to taste her sweet little pussy first." I gave them a wink, which earned me another scowl from Nico.

"Be careful what you share with her. I don't know how well we can trust her."

A couple hours later, I finally had a chance to go back and check on Valentina. I found her right where I left her, but she had showered and changed into a black cotton sundress that hugged her curves in a way that should be illegal. When I stepped inside, I stopped short at the sight of her. She was lying on her stomach reading a book that she must have pulled from the shelves I filled for her, and the dress was so short her ass was barely covered. As she turned to see me it rode up, displaying her rounded ass and a bit of a black lace thong she had on. The entire scene made my cock press even harder against the zipper of my jeans.

"Hey you," she said with a soft smile.

I couldn't help myself as my body moved in her direction. Her ass was calling for me and I couldn't contain my need to touch her. She watched with hooded eyes as I reached for her ankle, turned her body, and covered her with my own. She laughed and then gasped as I ground my hard dick into her covered pussy. The heat of her center was so intense I could feel it through both her panties and my jeans.

"La mia piccola bambola, he sent me to gather you for dinner, but your naughty little ass makes me want to eat you instead," I groaned into her ear as I rocked my hips forward again, only to be rewarded with her sweet, needy mouth on mine.

My mind was clouded with desire, and yet still I knew it wasn't time. Dante said he wanted her first, and I would respect that. I pushed myself up from the bed and reached for her hand, pulling her into a standing position as she whined at the loss of my body weight.

"Don't you think he'd understand if we were a little late?"

"No. Dante is nothing if not punctual, and family dinner is something that is a non-negotiable."

"Should I change?"

I looked down at her bare feet and tousled hair and smiled. The boys would be pleased at her slightly disheveled look.

"No."

I tucked her hand in mine and guided her down the long hallway that housed all of our private bedrooms. Valentina was quiet and observant the entire time. I could tell by the way she looked around that our home impressed her. However, she admired not only the furnishings but also the exits. I watched as her lips moved silently. She seemed to be counting, and I stopped us before we entered the main dining area.

"What are you doing?"

"Huh?"

"You were counting."

"I um, I count when I'm nervous," she said as she pulled her right hand from the pocket of her dress and opened it to show me the rocks I gathered for her.

"The doors are armed, just in case you were curious," I added before walking over to the table where Dante and Nico were already seated. The tension in the room was high so whatever they were talking about wasn't going well. When we walked in, both of their eyes darted to Valentina and a strange smile came over Nico that we rarely saw. Dante just sat there, being Dante. The stone-cold asshole that he loved to pretend he was.

"Boys, I present to you our little lady," I said, making a show of turning her in a circle as I attempted to ease the tension among everyone.

"Have a seat, Ragazzina."

I pulled out the chair next to mine and helped Valentina to sit. This was hopefully the first of many meals together and I didn't want it to be uncomfortable for her, but from the look on Dante's face, that wouldn't be easily avoided.

"How was your day?" he asked as he gestured for her plate and served her.

"It was fine. The room you have for me is wonderful. Thank you for that."

Dante tossed me a look of appreciation. Nico had made fun of me for weeks as delivery after delivery showed up. I wanted everything to be perfect for her, but designing a room and filling it with all the girlie things she would need was hard, since we knew so little about her at the time.

"Ares took great pride in picking everything out for you. We've had a place here for you here for a long time. It's good to know you are enjoying it."

Valentina's small hand made its way to my thigh, and she gave it a squeeze of appreciation.

"Will I be spending tomorrow there as well?"

"That depends."

"On what?"

"On if you followed my instructions this morning."

"I want to stay. There is nowhere else for me to go."

I reached for my wine and took a large sip. Her wanting to stay was good, but her reasoning was flawed. I knew the second I heard her, I knew Dante wouldn't stand for it.

"We aren't an orphanage. If the only reason you want to stay is because you have no place to go, then you will leave tonight. You can pack some items from your room and one of my men will take you to an apartment in the city. You can stay there until you get on your feet and find your own place."

Nico's anger was nearing a toxic level. He had stopped eating and began flipping around his favorite knife. Dante's only tell was the tapping of his fingers. Most didn't even notice it. Nico, on the other hand, played with weapons when he was pissed. Something I never understood as anything more than a scare tactic when we were younger, but after so many years, I learned it was more to calm him than anything else.

"That's not what I meant. I'm sorry if it came across that way. I don't want to stay only because I don't know where I'd go. I want to stay for you. I told you earlier that I have spent years preparing for this and if you'll still have me, I'd like to be yours."

CHAPTER EIGHT

VALENTINA

Fuck. Fuck. Fuck. I stepped right in it. I looked over at Dante, trying to gauge if he would accept my new answer to his question. Using appropriate wording with him was important. Everything I learned told me so, but now, sitting at a table with the man himself, I couldn't think clearly. Sure, I didn't want to leave because I really didn't have a clue where to go. Hell, I didn't even have a driver's license. It was yet another thing that my father felt I didn't need. But not wanting to leave was more than that. I didn't want to leave Dante. I spent most of my childhood fantasizing about what it would be like to be with a man like him. And then there was Ares... and Nico. Could I leave them? I had only been here since yesterday and emotions were running high, but they drew me to them both for different reasons. No one had told me we would all be together. They all just hinted at it. It should disgust me, but the idea of it was empowering.

They were all gorgeous, so a physical attraction wasn't in question. But my heart wanted Dante because it always had, and it wanted Nico because he needed me. I felt his eyes on me as he played with that knife he always had on him. The first time I noticed it was at a fundraiser my father took me to. I had been watching Dante all night, so it was hard to miss Nico and Ares. They were always at his side. As the speaker went on and on about some boring statistics, he sat there watching me, much like he was doing now, flipping a knife around between his fingers in a mesmerizing motion. I couldn't look away. The stories about Nico were whispers people told. Whispers of him butchering people and torturing others. They were more things that should have terrified me, but I wanted to know more. I wanted to know why.

I looked at Ares, who sat there with a glass of wine in his hand. He had grown quiet, and it made me uneasy. Of the three of them, he was the one who would fill the silence. The one to break the tension or entertain a crowd. He had his long hair pulled back tonight, and he didn't need his signature sunglasses inside. His eyes bore into me, trying to see something I didn't even know was there. Could I walk away from that? From my curiosity? From them? No. I knew in my heart I couldn't, even if my mind was trying to convince me to run. I always knew I wasn't normal, but my desire for these men made me wonder about my sanity more than anything else.

I turned back to Dante. He hadn't said a word since I spoke, and it didn't look as if he intended to. So I took a risk, one that would either work to my advantage, or get me thrown out. I pushed my chair back carefully and folded my napkin, placing it by my plate. I hadn't eaten much, but this fresh fear of rejection that had taken over caused me to lose my appetite. I took the few steps needed to close the space between Dante and I, and carefully, without a second thought, got to my knees. The silence of the room was deafening. Even the sound of Nico's knife clinking into his rings had quieted as I laid my head on Dante's lap and asked for forgiveness.

"I'm sorry, sir, I never meant to disrespect your offer. My words were hurtful, and I didn't mean it that way."

Dante had leaned back when I stood, allowing me the space I needed to lay my head down. My eyes were closed, but I could feel the muscles in his thigh tighten when I called him sir. Years ago, I met a young girl whose cousin had dated the three of them. She told stories of lust and chaos that had astonished me, but the more I thought about them, the more I realized that submission would be the way to Dante's heart. I didn't know much about sex, but one thing I did know was how to submit to a powerful man. Losing them now would be impossibly difficult, so I trusted my instincts and believed the rumors. If Dante wanted me to submit to him, then I that's what I would do. It wouldn't only be to gain a home to stay in, but to gain a lifetime of him, of them. The pet names they had given me already made my heart soar. Whether they spoke to me in Italian or English, it didn't matter. I knew they cared for me already and giving up control to them felt more natural than anything else I had ever decided in my life.

"Very good, Ragazzina," he said as his large hand came down and caressed my head as if I were a small child needing to be consoled, "I don't want to know where you learned this behavior, but I can tell you now, it is a great start. Now, take your seat next to Ares and finish your meal."

A collective sigh filled the room and my body melted into him, relaxing at his praise. It felt like a drug, the way his words rushed over my body and I worried that pulling myself from him to stand would be a struggle. I leaned back on my knees and dared to look up at him. His gaze captured me and it wasn't until I felt Ares' hand on my arm that I could move. He was standing behind me and the fact that I never heard him come for me just reinforced the turbulent effect Dante had on me. I took his hand and let him help me back into my seat.

"Valentina, there is something you need to understand."

I looked up at Dante, waiting for him to continue.

"If you stay, you will have me, but you will also have Nico and Ares. The three of us have plans for you, bigger than you may have imagined. I'm assuming, given what you just displayed, that you have heard of our... reputation. Let me assure you, everything you heard is true."

I sat there for a minute trying to compose myself. As I took deep breaths, I pressed my thighs together to quench the aching need between my legs. Then, without responding, I quietly finished my meal as the three men who would be my future continued their conversation as if what had just happened was completely normal.

The meal we ate was amazing, and I made a note to spend some time getting to know the kitchen staff when I was allowed to move about the house. The kitchen in my father's home was a safe haven for me. Our cook was a dear friend and over the years she would sneak treats to me, and let me help her prepare meals when my father was away. I loved to cook and always dreamed of what it would be like to own a restaurant one day.

When we finished eating, Nico pulled me from my chair and brought me to a sitting room that was attached to the main dining room. The entire Corsetti Estate was breath-taking. Everywhere I turned had hints of the old country, with artwork and pottery that must have been imported from Italy. They were things I had only seen in textbooks, and now I was walking down hallways and through rooms that were filled with art some people would only dream of. Nico handed me a glass of light brown liquor and motioned for me to drink. I did and then turned my nose up at the taste of it. I had the occasional glass of wine, but I was far from a drinker. He stood silently only a few feet away and pulled out a joint and lighter, sparking up right underneath a gorgeous painting of the Madonna and Child.

"It's the real thing," he said, pulling my attention back to him.

"What?"

"The painting. Ares has a thing for fancy art."

"But the original is in New York City, at the museum."

"Nope. Not anymore."

"But... how—"

"He is known for finding things... and when he finds something he likes, he takes it."

"But I saw it when my father's wife took me there for a luncheon. It was hanging at the MET."

"No, a reproduction is hanging at the MET. They just don't know it. Or maybe they do, but they don't want to admit they lost the original. Either way, it is what it is."

I was at a loss for words. They had stolen the Madonna and Child, and Nico acted as if it were no big deal. The Dark Kings were well known among the crime families of New York as the ruthless men, but I had no idea that stealing priceless art was on their list of things they did that skirted the law. I looked around the room I was sitting in. The dark decor and rich furnishings made me wonder how much of it was purchased and how much was just taken because Ares wanted it.

"Is there more?"

"I guess. Ares would be the one to ask. I'm not really into all the artsy shit he's into."

"I could see that."

Nico smiled slyly and crossed the room to where I was sitting on the couch. He took a seat and reached for my glass, placing it on the table in front of me. Before I knew it, he pulled me to him, lifting my leg and placing me so I was straddling his lap.

"Dante wanted me to wait for him but a little taste won't hurt anything," he said as he reached for my sundress and pulled it up over my head, exposing my breasts to him. I was too thin and felt subconscious over how small they were. Whenever I'd see women with Nico, they looked like supermodels. Swaying hips, large breasts, short dresses. What would he ever see in me?

"Stop," he grunted as he yanked my arms away from my body and held them behind my back with one hand. My shoulders pinched, but the pain subsided when his mouth came down and he sucked on my nipple for a brief moment. "Never hide yourself from us."

A groan escaped my mouth as he continued to suck and lick at my breasts, when his teeth came down over me my hips thrust forward and I was met with his hard cock beneath me. I rocked forward and back over him, pressing my clit into his length and feeling the heat rise within me faster than it ever had. I wanted this; I wanted Nico Marchesi more than anything. My body had taken on a mind of its own as it answered only to Nico. If only my actual mind would stop fighting me. This isn't normal. He's not your husband. What would Dante think? You haven't even married him and you're already going at it with his best friend? Then, as if my thoughts caused the man himself to materialize, the door opened and my body tensed at the sound of his voice.

"Well now, what do we have here?"

It wasn't Nico who responded, but Ares said, "Looks like our brother is having a hard time following tonight's rules."

Rules? They mentioned nothing about rules we need to follow.

Nico let go of my arms and grabbed my hips, forcing me to move over his hard cock again. "Ignore them. Come for me, la mia bella ragazza. Let me see it, just once before I give you to him."

The pleading sound in his voice undid me. I reached my arms around his neck and gave into the movements he was forcing on me. I could have taken over, began rocking my heated center over him again, but the forceful way he held me wasn't something I was willing to give up. He pressed me hard into him. My body was shaking with need.

"I can't hold on anymore," I gasped as he leaned forward and sucked on my neck. Then two things happened simultaneously. The deep timbre of Dante's voice hit my ears and ran through my body like electricity.

"Now, Ragazzina."

Before my body could relax enough to fall over the edge, the feel of Nico's teeth breaking the delicate skin on my neck ripped my climax from me. The pain was the tipping point, or maybe it was Dante's order. Either way, I was heading down an icy slope into a burning fire as wave after wave of ultimate pleasure hit my body. The light tingling feeling I would get from pleasuring myself was nothing compared to the feeling that shook my body in that moment. As it slowly subsided, I felt weak, needy and unable to hold myself up. That I was still wearing panties, and three of the hottest men in New York City had watched me as I screamed out my release wasn't lost on me. My mind screamed that I was a fool, but with Nico still holding on to me, it was easy to push those thoughts away.

I collapsed onto him and felt his tongue lathe over the place where he bit into me. But the next set of hands I felt weren't his at all. It was Ares, I could already recognize his touch. His fingers danced up my spine until they moved my long dark hair away from my neck. I heard him let out a sigh before he pulled me from Nico and into his arms.

"That's going to leave a bruise, you know."

"That was my plan."

"Come with me, La mia piccola bambola. Nico's already made a mess of you and the night hasn't even begun."

I dropped my head onto Ares' shoulder as he walked from the room. I could have easily walked, but there was something nice about being treated as his little doll. The endearment wasn't lost on me. I learned Italian when I learned English and that each of them had their own name for me in our native language made my heart soar.

Ares didn't take me to his room, but to Dante's. He laid me down on the bed and he slid my panties from me. I watched as he lifted them to his nose and took a deep breath of my scent. His eyes closed, and he groaned before he stuffed them into his pocket.

"He said he wanted you first. But soon you'll be mine."

"First?" I dared to ask.

"There will be a day we can take you together, a day I pray comes soon. But tonight, since this will be your first time, you will be with Dante. Nico and I won't leave you, but he will be your first."

I nodded, but said nothing.

"Is this really what you want, Valentina? All of us. Everything that comes along with it?"

"It is." Even with Dante standing in the doorway, I knew in my heart I was telling Ares the truth. It may not make sense to many people, but for the first time in my life, I felt like I was in the exact place that I was always meant to be.

CHAPTER NINE

DANTE

I knew Ares had his concerns over Valentina, but the tone of his voice when he asked her again if she wanted to stay was surprising. We had talked about this day since we found out about her. Then spent years hunting her down and figuring out the best way to get her here, where she belonged. He did most of that work. Ares deserved this life with her just as much as any of us did. In fact, he may deserve it more.

I stood in the doorway and watched quietly as he leaned over her and placed a gentle kiss on her lips. Her arms came up around him and he had to pull himself back from her to stand and move away. He took a seat at the small table in the corner of my room. The same one Valentina enjoyed her breakfast at earlier in the day. I approached the bed as she watched me carefully. We hadn't spent much time together, and in truth, they had filtered the only things she knew about me. Her asshole father's stories and the rumors she heard from the other families were all she had to go on. Even though I had always known she would be my wife, I never planned for anything more with her than sex. Ares and Nico could fulfill any other needs she had. The love between a man and a woman caused nothing but destruction, especially in our world. But looking down at her, naked and nervous in my bed, made my heart jump in a way I hadn't expected.

I heard Nico come in and take a seat with Ares, but I couldn't pull my eyes away from my little girl. She was stunning.

"I will give you one more chance, Valentina. Is this what you want from us or not?"

"It is," she whispered as I unbuttoned my vest and dress shirt that I had worn today with my suit. Her eyes were glued to me as I continued to undress. I didn't hide my erection. I wanted her, wanted this for longer than I could remember. Tonight, I would initiate our little one into a wonderful world of debauchery, and the excitement running through me was stronger than the electric ropes Ares liked to play with.

"We will have rules, Ragazzina. Rules that you will need to follow and if you don't, you will be disciplined. Do you understand?"

"Yes, sir."

Damn, that sounded good. "Tonight, you will no longer wonder what it will be like to be with a man. I will do my best not to hurt you, but we need to get past this so we can move on to more adventurous things. Do you have questions for me?"

Valentina's eye contact broke away from me and she looked over at the table with my brothers. "Will they watch, or can they touch me?"

Her curiosity was getting the better of her. I had planned for distance while I was with her, but from the look in her eyes, it made me think she wanted more.

"Would you like them in bed with us?"

"I think I would."

I looked over at the two of them, but they were already on their feet, undressing as they walked to my bed. The beds in each of our rooms were larger than normal. Years ago, we had to have them custom made, but now they are sold as family beds. When Ares found them for our penthouse in the city, I couldn't help but laugh. We were certainly a family, just not the kind the designers intended.

They had both stripped down to only their boxer briefs and Ares slid on one side of Valentina while Nico moved to the other. They both turned into her and Ares kissed her fiercely while Nico played with her breasts. It was a beautiful sight to be seen. I knew she was already slick from Nico's foreplay, but since this was her first time, I wanted to take every precaution necessary. I went to my nightstand and pulled condoms and a bottle of lube. She pulled away from Ares and looked in my direction.

"I'm um... I have an IUD. They got it for me when I turned eighteen in case you didn't want children and I haven't been with anyone, so I'm clean."

I looked down at the box of condoms in my hand and looked back at her.

"Are you sure?"

"Yes. I want to feel you inside of me. The way it was always supposed to be."

Nico's arm wrapped around her center, pulling her tighter to him as he pressed his hips forward and whispered something into her ear that turned her a gorgeous shade of pink. I put the condoms back and went to her. I slipped out of my boxers and took my cock in my hand. She watched me with wide, hungry eyes while I jerked it a few times. This woman was going to be the death of me. I crawled up to her from the bottom of the bed and stopped myself at that sweet little pussy of hers. As I pressed her legs apart, Ares and Nico secured them, holding her open for me. I didn't waste any time. My tongue hit her clit as I pressed a finger deep inside her. She was so tight it felt as if she would strangle my cock. I looked up to find Nico's mouth on hers and Ares pinching and rolling her nipples between his fingers as he sucked on her neck. Her hips lifted and she let out a little gasp when I pulled out and added another. With two fingers deep inside of her, I stroked her and sucked her little clit. The noises coming from her were like music to my ears. Our little virgin, my Ragazzina, was finally right where she was supposed to be. Between the three of us, where no other person had ever fit so perfectly.

Her breathing was coming harder and faster. She couldn't focus on Nico any more and had reached forward, gripping my hair with her hands, holding me in the place where she wanted me. She thrust her hips forward as Nico devoured her neck and Ares sucked her breast into his mouth. The orgasm that hit seemed to shock her. Valentina's eyes went wide as her lips parted and then the tension that came over her snapped and she tried her hardest to push me away from her pulsing clit.

"More," I grunted as Nico pulled her hands away from me. She had gone from holding me to her, to pushing me away in a matter of seconds. I grinned to myself as I tortured her oversensitive clit and looked up to find Nico had one arm held over her head and Ares had the other. If I thought she was beautiful before, nothing compared to the sight of them restraining her for me. I continued on as she cried out to stop.

"No more, please, I can't."

"You can, and you will," Nico growled since I couldn't be bothered to pull myself away from her pussy. I pressed three fingers into her this time, the stretch making her whine in discomfort, but her hips pushed into me with each thrust. Her third climax of the night didn't take long. I needed her full sated before we began. None of us were small, and she was so tight. It would be uncomfortable for her if we hadn't prepared her properly, and I wanted her memories of tonight to be nothing but amazing. Her body shook again as her head thrashed from side to side. She cried out my name when the first wave hit her and her eyes rolled back. Her body went slack in my brothers' grasp and when I felt the last few contractions of her inner walls around my fingers, I slowly pulled out and pressed them into her mouth. She hadn't even opened her eyes, just took them in and sucked like the good little girl that she was.

"Very good, Ragazzina. You are very impressive," I whispered into her ear as I covered her body with mine. It was time. The moment I'd been waiting for since the day she turned eighteen. Having her under my body was more amazing than anything I could have ever imagined. She was small, too small really, but between the three of us, she was just as Ares called her. Our perfect little doll. Her eyes opened slowly, and she smiled up at me with a sultry smile I'd never forget.

"Are you ready?"

She nodded her head, but I needed more. "Tell me what you need."

"I need you."

"How?"

Her cheeks pinked, and she lowered her gaze. Ares and Nico's hands hadn't left her, and she did well not allowing them to distract her, but her eyes slipped quickly to Ares and I reached for her chin, and pulled her gaze back to mine.

"Tell me Valentina, I want to hear your words. Tell me exactly what you want from me tonight."

"I want you to fuck me."

"How?"

"In every way possible. I've only ever imagined what tonight would be like, and this has already surpassed anything I dreamed of." I let go of her chin and let her glance at Nico and Ares. "I want all of you, but I don't know what to do. I want to learn what you like, how to please you, and how to make you come."

"Very good. Now relax your body for me."

She held Ares' hand and reached her other to my chest, placing it over my heart. I knew it was racing at her touch and I could only imagine what she was thinking as she looked down to see what would come next. I slipped my finger between her folds and stroked her clit a couple of times until she opened for me. She lifted both of her legs and gave herself up as a sweet offering of pleasure. I reached for the lube, not willing to risk any friction or discomfort I could avoid, and coated myself thoroughly, slipping a small amount into her center as she squirmed under my touch.

"This may hurt at first but it can't be helped. I will go slow until you are settled and comfortable, then I will show you how I can make you come all over my cock."

The little groan that came from her nearly made me lose control. Instead of plowing into her like the animal I felt I was, I slowly, inch by inch, made my way into her tight center.

"So fucking beautiful, and all mine," I grunted as I pushed further. Her body tensed and I watched as Ares whispered calming words into her ear and Nico rubbed small circles into the soft skin on her chest. These men would do anything for the woman beneath me and if we could get past the shit her family caused, our future would be remarkable. I leaned forward and captured her mouth with mine, and loved the way her lips molded to me. It was as if she were made for me. I tasted her, opening her up to everything I wanted and then pressed forward the last bit until I broke through what she had held precious for so many years.

She let out a small yelp of pain that I had expected but it still crushed me I had hurt her in a way she didn't desire. "Relax your body, Ragazzina. Take a deep breath."

Valentina followed my command and as much as it killed me, I didn't move a muscle while she adjusted to my size.

"You're okay, La mia piccola bambola. We've got you. That's the hardest part, now it will be nothing but pleasure. I promise you," Ares said to her as he stroked her hair.

"I need to move now, little one," I warned, then slid myself out of her and then back in. I went slow and didn't vary my movements much. The repetition helped her settle quickly, and when a smile came over her beautiful face, I knew she had seen the light. I increased my pace, trying my hardest not to slam into her. The level of control I needed at this moment was more than anything I had experienced before. This was why it had to be me. Nico would have killed her and Ares, although more considerate, lacked the control needed to ensure she wasn't hurt.

"You're good, little one," I whispered as I slipped my hand under her ass and rocked harder into her hips, being sure to press myself into her clit with the upward movement. Her eyes opened wide, and she reached for me.

"More like that," she panted out as she pulled me closer. We kept going as her body opened to me more and more. It was as if we were the only two people in the world. Her eyes darted from staring up at me, then back to where we were connected. She was watching everything as if she were trying her hardest to lock every detail into memory.

It was getting harder and harder to hold off, and I needed her to come for me. I was desperate to see it again. I ground my hips into her as her nails dug into my biceps. The pain was a pleasant distraction as her climax began to slowly work its way up through her. I could feel her walls tightening around me and her breath came out in sharp breaths. I held her tightly to me and Ares and Nico's hands never left her. Every time I hit that one spot deep within her, she would let out the sweetest sounding cry.

"That's it, let go," I growled into her ear and the second I did, her body gave way. She yelled out her release and the sound of it broke down every ounce of control I had displayed. My movements became rough, hard, and deliberate as the sensations ran up my spine and exploded in the back of my mind.

"Mine," I grunted as I emptied myself into her, and with one final thrust, I looked into her eyes and corrected myself.

"Ours."

CHAPTER TEN

VALENTINA

I couldn't breathe. Well, maybe I could because I wasn't dead, but it felt like I had just run a race. My body went limp in their hold and I didn't even bother trying to move. Dante was still inside me. His cock twitched, which made my inner walls tighten around him again. I never imagined how amazing it would feel to have him inside of me. I heard terrible stories from some girls about how painful it would be and that the first time was never good, but none of that applied to me. Sure, it hurt at first, not that I had much to compare to, but Dante seemed huge. Laying between Nico and Ares while he made love to me made it impossible for me not to enjoy every second. I closed my eyes and let out a small laugh. The books I read were nothing compared to the real thing.

"Is something funny?" Ares said softly into my ear.

"Someone needs to write a book about this, because the stuff I read didn't do it justice," I mumbled the best I could. They fried my brain with lust and the only thing I could think about was how terribly wrong my school books got things.

Dante's body was still over mine, and I felt him tense and pull away.

"No, don't," I begged, grasping him tighter in an effort to pull him back to me.

"We need to get you cleaned up."

"But I don't want you to leave."

"I'm not going far. Stay with the boys. I'll start a bath for you and be back."

When he pulled out, I felt an emptiness that I didn't know I had before. I hated it in that moment, but what I hated more was that I could feel Ares and Nico's hard cocks pressed against me and there wasn't anything I could do about it. I moved my hands from where they lay over my stomach and, in a half-hearted attempt, reached for both. Nico grunted and pressed himself into my hand, where Ares let out a hiss as if I had burned him.

"Is it over?" I asked quietly, while trying to figure out what this all meant and what would come next.

Ares shifted his hips so I couldn't reach him. "For now, yes."

"But what about the both of you? I can't just leave you like this."

Nico's lips reached my neck, and I groaned as he bit my skin lightly.

"Dante's right, you need some time to recover. A bath will do you good." Ares answered, but Nico seemed to have other plans.

His fingers made their way down my body and he toyed with the curls between my legs before slipping one finger over my clit. It was painful, but I didn't dare push him away. I ached in places I didn't know possible, but I still wanted him. I wanted them both.

"Please. I need you," I said, rolling over toward Nico. Ares seemed to be a lost cause, insisting on following Dante's orders. Nico, on the other hand, and taken advantage of the fact I was still lying naked next to him in bed. I moaned as his lips caught mine. His tongue twirled, tasted and owned me in ways Dante hadn't. He was more forceful, more determined than the other two. When his head slipped to the side and he bit down on the lobe of my ear, I realized I would get more than I bargained for with him. I let out a gasp as Ares moved to get up. The loss of his heat behind me, or maybe it was the dangerous things Nico was doing to my body, caused me to shiver.

"Nico, enough," I heard Dante's voice as Nico's body froze in place.

"Later, you will be mine,." he growled in my ear as he pulled his body from mine. I laid back on the bed, trying to catch my breath as a shadow came over me. Dante had come as promised, and he didn't look pleased.

"What did I tell you?"

"That you were coming back for me."

"I wouldn't have thought I needed to be detailed in my instructions to you."

"I'm sorry. I just…" As I trailed off, I realized the room had emptied, and it was just Dante and myself. It shouldn't make me as nervous as it did, but with Ares and Nico gone, I was the only person he focused on. I had disobeyed him and we both knew it. It wasn't intentional, but the rules and guidelines were all blurry right now. He had asked me where I wanted the other two men, but he hadn't explicitly said not to touch them. I sat up on the side of the bed.

"You didn't say I couldn't touch them."

"I didn't think I needed to."

"Will it always be like this? You controlling my relationships with each of you?"

"I'm not—" I watched as he tapped his fingers on the side of his leg before continuing. "No, I will not control your relationships with them, but I won't let you make decisions that are not good for you just to benefit any of us."

"Wouldn't I be the one to know if I'm making a poor decision?"

"Not always. This is all new for you. You're going to have to trust that with some of our... lifestyle... you will need our advice and guidance until you learn more."

I was uneasy with him towering over me as we spoke. When I moved, I could feel the soreness between my legs even more than when I had been laying with Nico. The ache was the best kind of pain, but the face I made must have said otherwise. Dante's features changed immediately but rather than concern, he looked even more upset with me.

"I hurt you."

"No. I'm not hurt. Really, I'm fine."

"I told you this could happen. I told you I'd come back to take care of you, but you couldn't wait, could you?"

"Dante, I —"

I couldn't finish my thought, which was probably a good thing, since I didn't know what to say. He reached forward and scooped me up from the bed. After a few steps to his master bath, he was lowering the both of us into a huge marble tub that could easily sit ten people. Or three oversized men and me. I smiled to myself at the thought.

"Do you find this entertaining?" he asked, jarring me from my mini fantasy of what we could do in here.

"No. I'm sorry. My mind was just wandering."

"I don't like that you apologize so much. I will ensure you behave in a scene or when we are out, but at home, I want you to speak freely."

"Even if you won't like what I have to say?"

"Yes. If I understand your past correctly, your punishments and isolation stemmed from you speaking your mind. It won't be like that in our future. You are a powerful woman, Valentina, and we will grow to respect your opinion as much as each other's."

I looked up at Dante and was at a loss for words. No one ever cared about my thoughts on anything and now, here was this man who was known for his stubbornness and wrath, yet he was offering me something I never expected.

"My mind was wandering at the thoughts of what the four of us could do here," I said, gesturing at the tub.

Dante's smile was rare, and I cherished it at that moment. "Our little virgin is turning into a vixen."

He leaned down and kissed me, then continued to quietly wash my body. It felt strange allowing this much intimacy between us, but I kept telling my mind this was what we had waited for. This was what we dreamed of. I forced myself to relax in his arms, but when he brought the soft washcloth between my legs, I couldn't help but squirm. It hurt and then without warning his fingers were swirling my clit. I should be done, spent, finished. But I could feel the rise in my body again. Would I ever get enough of him? Of them? I felt so dirty today as I laid in my room and fantasized about what life would be like with them. Now before my mind could catch up with my actions, here I was ready to come all over this man's hands.

"Dante, please."

"Please what?"

"I need more."

"Ask nicely, Ragazzina."

"Please, make me come."

He pulled his hand away from me and I all but screamed out my frustration. I sat up and put some space between us, turning on him, ready to rage, but the look he had on his face shut me right up.

He reached for my hands and pulled me roughly back to him, splashing water all over the floor. He pulled my hips forward, and I was straddling him. His cock was hard again, and he had a hold of me by my mess of wet hair. He tilted my head back just enough to make me uncomfortable, but not enough to cause pain. I looked at him through my slanted eyes. My body was on fire and it took everything not to roll my hips forward, giving into the uncontrollable need coursing through me.

"It's time for you to learn a few things," he said in a voice so deadly I didn't dare speak a word, "Your only job in this world is to follow my instructions. They are as follows. You will eat regularly and drink plenty of water. You will never leave this house without one of us by your side. You will take care of what is mine. Do you know what's mine, Valentina?"

"Me," I whispered.

"Yes, you. If you are hurt, bruised, or bloody from play, then I want to know. You will use a number system to keep yourself safe with us. Especially with Nico. One means you are fine, three means things are getting more intense, five means stop. You're a smart girl, I'm sure you can work out the rest," he said as his other hand held me down and his hips thrust forward, pressing his cock between my folds just enough to tease me.

"When I tell you that you have had enough for the night, then I expect you to listen to me. You were a virgin little one. I do not take what you have given me lightly and I will not allow you to run to the others tonight for more. Any questions?"

I had a million, but how could I bother him with it all now? Dante went from the loving man who was washing my hair and encouraging me to share my thoughts to someone who seemed ready to strangle me. I'm not sure why that turned me on so much, but it did. Both sides of him made me want him, but it was clear I had gone too far this time. I was finally getting answers to some of what I had wondered, but it wasn't everything. I needed Ares. He was easier to talk to. He could help me navigate this mess. But my heart called for Nico. He wanted me. I know he did, and I didn't fulfil that need for him tonight.

"Will Ares and Nico be allowed back tonight?"

"They were never told to leave."

"But they did."

Dante didn't say another word. Instead of talking, he let go of my hair and reached for a bottle of conditioner. He lathered my hair, running his fingers through it, which didn't help my current state of arousal. When he seemed pleased I was clean enough, he stood and reached a hand out for me. I climbed the three steps from the sunken tub, holding his hand and he wrapped me in a huge white towel.

"My clothes are all in my room."

"You don't need clothes to sleep. In fact, from now on, anytime you are in my room you will undress at the door. I will not have you hide yourself from me like you did with Nico. Until you gain confidence in yourself and your body, you will not be permitted to cover yourself while here."

"But what about the people you have working here?"

"What about them?"

"They'll see me."

Dante didn't say anything, but instead I watched him hide a small smile. There was something else going on with him. He wasn't letting on, and I was bound and determined to find out what it was. I sat on the bench in his bathroom as he brushed out my wet hair and then followed him back into the bedroom. Each of our rooms appeared to be the size of small apartments. I hadn't seen much of Ares', but Nico's, Dante's and mine were all similar. Dante's was larger and decorated to his style, but they all had a sleeping area, sitting area with a bar and a private bath. I looked around to take in what I missed earlier.

The floors were a dark wood, and the decor matched a more modern style than I would have expected. The walls were painted a dark gray and his bed was as huge as mine and Nico's. I wasn't a complete idiot. Sure, I didn't see a lot outside of my father's home, but I knew these beds weren't normal. It made me wonder where they came from and why they were all here. I'm sure they had other partners they shared but did they all live here with them at one point? Did other women sleep in my room?

He pulled back the covers that had appeared to have been changed while we were in the bathroom and I crawled in towards the middle of the bed.

"Go to sleep Ragazzina," he said as he leaned over and placed a kiss on my forehead.

"Wait, where are you going?"

"I have work that I need to get done."

"So you're leaving me in here."

"For now, yes."

"Aren't you tired?"

He tilted his head to the side as if just now considering this was the time of day to sleep. "I suppose I am. At least more than normal. I don't sleep as much as the others. I'll send them in to stay with you until I'm finished. Good night, little one."

I was at a loss for words. After everything that had happened between us and then the time in the bath, I had assumed he would lie down with me and sleep. But he was still Don Dante Corsetti and his businesses never rested. I laid there for a while, staring up at the ceiling and wondering what my father and Angelo Costa were thinking about. Dante had said everything was done, that there was no house to return to. Did that mean they thought I was dead? I needed some answers from Dante... or maybe Ares, and I really needed to call my father in the morning to make sure he was okay. I told Dante I still loved him and that wasn't a lie. He was my father and the only person I really had. My cousin had to be worried sick, too. Tomorrow I'd work on getting them to agree with me having a phone. Tonight, I was going to close my eyes and relish in the fact that even though I didn't have Dante laying with me tonight, there were two gorgeous men who had just cracked open the door to the room and quietly crawled into bed on either side of me.

CHAPTER ELEVEN

ARES

Nico and Dante left early to meet with the Costas, which left me with Valentina. Nico was pissed I was the one home with her again, but my work for the family consisted primarily of computer work, so I was normally the here anyway. Only on the days I visited the shop or had to deal with some of my contacts did I need to leave. The guys left her sleeping, and I relished in the moments of holding her a while longer before starting my day. Her soft body tucked into my side made it difficult to pull myself away.

When I got up and dressed, I set off to get breakfast prepared. I wanted to spend some time with Valentina and get to know things about her I couldn't learn from the profile I had built over the years. By the time I made it back to the bedrooms, I found her dressed and sitting on her bed.

"Hey, what are you doing?"

"Just finishing this book. I've never read anything like this before."

"Ah, The Great Gatsby... one of the classics."

"To be honest, I was never much of a reader. The tutors I had were fans of boring educational nonfiction stuff. Once in a while I'd luck out and it would be a biography."

"Do you like reading biographies? I can order you some."

"I do, well I did. Now I'm wondering if fiction is the way to go," she said as she let out a little laugh, "I always loved how messy people's lives were, which is why a good biography always appealed to me. The characters in this book seem so real it's unbelievable. Are they all like this?"

"What, books? No. Some are better than others. I've enjoyed reading on and off throughout my life, but I'm more of a mood reader than anything else. If I find something I like, then I find more of it."

"I could see that about you," she gave me a small smile, and I wanted to skip breakfast completely and bury myself in her.

I shook my head. "You can't keep looking at me like that or you will starve."

"I'm more worried about my lack of caffeine than my lack of food. I used to love helping out in the kitchen at my father's. Do you think that's something I could do here?"

"I don't see why not."

"Madeline taught me so much when I was young. She would even sneak me treats. I used to daydream about owning or working in a restaurant one day. One she could come to and eat all of the recipes she taught me to make."

The pain in my chest knowing what I knew kept me from addressing her comments. "Come on, we'll eat outside in the courtyard."

"You don't think Dante will be mad, do you? I know he wants me to stay in here."

"It's fine. Just don't wander off or I'll end up getting in trouble again."

"Did you already?" she asked as we made our way down the long hallway and into the main part of the house.

"I guess getting in trouble isn't the best way to explain it. Dante is more the brooding type when he's annoyed with me and Nico. He makes faces, slams cabinets and storms off, but it's not like he scolds us like small children."

She laughed, "What did you get in trouble for, anyway?"

"Did you forget already that you stormed out of your room the other night on a hunt for Nico? It pissed him off. I didn't lock us in and you left."

"Well, it pissed me off that you two thought it was okay to sedate a full-grown man who wasn't doing anything wrong."

When we got outside, I pulled out a chair for her to sit. The staff had already set up our meal, so I reached forward and poured her a cup of coffee before taking my seat and sipping my espresso.

"It's really beautiful out here."

"Now it is."

Valentina shook her head in my direction. "That is so corny."

"What can I say? I speak what's on my mind and if I find something beautiful, I say it."

"Or take it?"

"What do you mean by that?"

"Nico told me about the Madonna and Child. How did you even pull something like that off?"

I smiled, "Okay, you're right, when I find something beautiful, I take it."

I reached for her hand and placed a kiss on her palm. The soft looks she gave me were addictive, and I sat wondering what else I could do for her to get them.

"So you're not going to tell me?"

"How I got the painting? No. I enjoy leaving a little mystery in the air."

We ate in a comfortable silence. It was nice being with a woman who didn't need to talk constantly. It's not that I didn't want to hear what she had to say, but some people just speak to hear their own voice.

"You're quiet today."

"I guess I just don't have a lot to say. But you're quiet too."

"Outside of the house, I'm the one who gets stuck schmoozing people and playing the game of politics that comes with what we do. When I'm home, I finally get to turn that all off. It's nice."

"I'm sure it is. When my father or stepmother took me out, I'd have to play this role of the perfect little princess. It was forced and annoying. As soon as I closed the door to my bedroom at night, I felt like a load of bricks had been lifted from my shoulders. It really is tiring pretending you are someone you're not. I know why I did it, but why do you do it?"

"Someone needs to. Dante can't always play nicely and Nico is a time bomb ready to go off at any given moment."

"Was he always that way?"

"No. Not when we were younger. Actually, you'd be surprised to know he was always the goofball. The one playing pranks and making everyone laugh. He spent more time in trouble than he spent out of it just because he thrived off the laughter of others."

"Really? You're right, I never would have known." She looked off into the distance for a minute before looking back at me. "What happened to him?"

I should have known she'd want to know more. "It's not really my story to tell. Something happened when we were in our early twenties. We were in Italy taking care of business for Dante's father and... well, something happened there that changed him."

The tears in her eyes were surprising. I wouldn't have expected she'd care for any of us so deeply when we had only been together for a couple of days.

"So, tell me about you," I asked, trying to change the subject.

"There isn't much to tell. I lived a pretty secluded life until now, and I'm not even certain that's changing."

"It is. It will. Dante just needs some time to get used to everything."

"You mean me?"

"It was hard on him, Valentina. It was hard on all of us not knowing what happened to you for so long. Much like they prepared you to be his wife, he had always known in his heart you were his. When that didn't happen, things got difficult."

"What about you and Nico? Was I always part of your plan, too?"

"Not always, but it was only a year after Dante learned about you we decided the only way to make things work was with all of us. The rumors about some of our past encounters had already made their way to your father, and Dante blamed himself for that. For the longest time, he thought that was the reason your father wouldn't follow through with his promise."

"That wasn't it. Or at least I doubt it was. He pushed me around like a pawn in a game. Have you talked to him? Does he know I'm here and okay?"

"No."

"Dante said the house was gone, burned down. Does that mean he thinks I'm dead?"

"I know you have questions, but there will be a better time for the answers."

She looked away, then reached for her coffee. I couldn't imagine what she was thinking in that moment, but I certainly would not be the one to tell her what happened.

"Can I make a call today? Not to my father, just to my cousin Mario. I want him to know I'm okay and I can trust him to keep it to himself. If there is some reason you don't want my dad to know where I am, then I'll tell him not to say anything."

"I can't do that."

"Can't or won't?"

"Both. There are much larger things at play here, Valentina. We need to get through the next couple of weeks, and then we can talk about any ongoing relationships you can maintain."

"What does that even mean?"

"Finish up and then we need to head back. The guys should be back here soon and they will want to talk to me."

I could sense her annoyance. It was clear she felt as if she could ask me the things Dante didn't want her to know, but I still wasn't ready to tell her everything. Even though she stayed, I wouldn't be surprised if she tried to run when she learned the truth about the other night, the truth about what we did. Maybe it was a mistake spending this time with her. I wanted to move forward with things, but if she continued to press me about every little detail, I wouldn't be able to. It would hurt too much when she left.

CHAPTER TWELVE

NICO

I didn't want to be at this stupid fucking meeting. I wanted to be inside Valentina but instead of sinking my cock deep into her core, Dante yanked me off of her and told me to shower and dress. This was a three-piece suit kind of meeting, and I hated getting dressed up. Armani, it seemed to be the lesser of two evils with the suits Ares bought for me. The others were cut too close to my body and made me even more uncomfortable. Since I was told to make sure I was presentable, I had fewer knives on me than I'd like. Guns were fine, and I never left the house without them, but killing someone with a knife was a feeling that you never forgot. I didn't believe in killers who compartmentalized everything. If you take someone's life, you should remember it. Remember them. All in all, today was shit, and it wasn't even noon.

"We're so sorry for your loss," I heard Dante droning on with pleasantries, "But I'm not sure what the death of your friend has to do with me."

In New York City, we were at one of our properties. We rarely slept here, but used it for meetings just like this. We lived at Villa Corsetti, and all of us preferred it that way. It kept a certain distance between work and home life.

"As you know, it wasn't just the death of a friend but also the loss of my future wife."

"Really? I hadn't heard," Dante said, as his hands curled tightly around the arms of his chair.

"It was an arrangement made just recently. I believe you knew his daughter, Valentina?"

Dante was pissed, and I couldn't blame him. "Yes, but wasn't she a young girl?"

"She was, but the younger the better in my eyes. Lets you train them up real nice." I stepped forward, ready to plunge the knife I was playing with into the sick fuck's throat, but was stopped by a hand from one of his guards. Dante didn't even flinch. This is why he and I hold two very different jobs in the family.

"So, Angelo, how exactly can I help you then?"

"There are rumors. That she may have made it out of the fire. Her room was empty and if that's the case, then I would like your permission to hire some of your men to find her."

"My men?"

"Yes. I have an upcoming auction and would like this settled beforehand. I approached a security firm, Calvano

Security, but they aren't looking to bring on any new clients."

I laughed, knowing damn well who he was talking about. The men he was contacted were all military veterans. They did a lot of private security for families and friends of people who had been in the service. I remembered stories of Angelo being in the Army but if my memory was correct, they dishonorably discharged him. Not that a dishonorable discharge would keep them from working with him. They worked in the gray aspects of the law and had been known to do whatever it takes to get the results they were looking for. No, the real reason they wouldn't work with the Costas was because Dante told them not to. There were quite a few families in the city who we kept a close eye on, and they were one of them. Bringing down Romano wouldn't solve the trafficking problem, but it would slow things down. The Calvano Security Firm had worked a handful of trafficking cases in the city and we asked for a meeting as soon as we learned what was happening.

"So what makes you think I'd assist in this search of yours?"

"I know your men are some of the best. I've spoken to Valentina's cousin, and he's desperate for information about her. They were very close and if she's out there, we would both like to make sure she's okay. If she's not, then the closure is important to the both of us."

Dante sat and listened to the man's plea. Although plea is a pretty strong word for what was going on. He was trying to appear desperate for help, but we both knew it was a front. Angelo Costa was an ass of a man. If he was coming to us for help, then there was something else he was trying to gain. It would just take time to figure out what that is.

"What will we get in exchange for helping you? My men aren't just men for hire. They are in my regular employ and working for someone else will take them from the work they do for me."

"I understand that, and considered what to offer you. Money of course, is always an option but a business deal could sweeten the pot, as they say?"

"What kind of business?"

"As you know, with Romano gone, that leaves a hole in the ownership group of our latest endeavor. I know he had spoken to you and at the time you declined, but I'm here to offer more. A sixty/forty split. Forty percent of all profits go to you, and my team will run and operate it. No need for any additional work, just a check for you to collect after each auction."

"And if I said no to Romano, what makes you think I will work with you?"

"I know he offered you less. I'm willing to increase the split to bring on a partner of... your caliber."

"No."

"Don Corsetti, I promise you this will be a valuable partnership. It has already exceeded anything we had ever thought was possible."

"Angelo, are you here grieving the loss of a fiancée and friend or are you here looking for a business partner? Because in either situation, I don't see a reason for my family to be involved with you."

"I have a son. He needs a family to work for. One that would keep him safe."

This idiot was trying way too hard. Something was up and it wasn't appealing in the slightest. There was a reason I don't do these meetings with Dante. It's because I don't have Ares' patience for the political bullshit. If it were up to me, he'd already be dead and we would enjoy a nice meal in Little Italy, but no.

"You really need to figure out your priorities," Dante said as he went to stand, "My men will see you out."

"Wait! Please. I... I'm serious about my son."

"You may be, but working for my family is not an option. And as for looking for your former fiancée, I'll consider it and Ares will be in touch. I don't want part of your and Romano's business. If I decide to help, then I will determine what the payment will be and when it will be made."

Dante turned from the table and left the room. I followed while two of our men walked in and escorted the asshole and his men out.

"What a fucking dick," I said as soon as the door closed to our office that we kept here.

"He's up to something."

"Of course he is. Whenever is he not up to something?"

"It's going to be a problem, and I don't want to deal with it right now. I'll have Ares set up surveillance, and we will see what he's really up to."

"His kid is a problem. I've seen him at some fights. They have banned him from most because of his lack of control."

"Like you should talk."

"At least I can buy my way back in when I want. This kid is a junkie and broke. If it were possible to tarnish the

Costa name any more than Angelo has, then he did. No one will get near him."

"Is the son a risk I need to worry about?"

"No, he's still young and stupid. But I agree Angelo is up to something."

"I'll have Ares put some guys on it. I want to know what his plans are and it's easier having first-hand knowledge."

"Can we leave now?"

"You can. I need Ares at the club tonight, which will leave you with Valentina. I don't have to explain to you how disappointed I will be if I come home and find her hurt."

"Hurt how?"

"You know what I mean, Nico. I need to know I can trust you not to do anything that will scare her off."

"You're just as much of an ass as Costa."

I left him sitting there in on his royal throne of dickery. Today wasn't a time to pick a fight with him though. I needed Valentina more and the fact that I had over an hour's drive back to her was already pissing me off.

By the time I got to the villa, it was late afternoon and Ares was quick to leave. Something seemed to bother him, but he wasn't talking about it and I wasn't really the type who gave a shit. I found Valentina locked in her room, just like she was supposed to be. Instead of kicking back and relaxing, she was pacing around like a caged beast. The idea of her locked up in there just waiting for us did things to me that I shouldn't be proud of. When I opened the door, she hadn't stopped pacing. She was talking to herself as well. Murmuring some utter nonsense. I closed the door behind me and watched as she continued to move throughout the room without even glancing up. She was lost. Stuck in a way I understood all too well, and I needed it to stop. As she rounded the corner of her bed, I walked forward right into her path and it wasn't until she was inches from running into me that she jolted to a stop.

"Nico."

I lifted my eyebrows in recognition of my name, but didn't give her anything else to work with. I've learned with time the only reason to stop the silence is if the words you have to say will make it better and right now, I had nothing to improve her situation.

"I didn't hear you come in."

"I know."

"Is Dante back too?"

"Do you want him to be back?"

"Do you always answer questions with other questions?"

"If there is information I need, then yes."

She looked behind me at the closed door and then around the room.

"We're alone."

"You are doing a pretty good job of stating the obvious."

"I'm sorry, I'm just… I'm getting a little anxious here."

"You said you wanted to stay. You knew the conditions of that agreement. Do you want to leave now?"

"No, no, it's nothing like that."

"Then what is it?"

"I need to know what's going on. You all say my life won't be like it was there, but it's feeling that way. I want… I think I want to talk to my dad. Let him know I'm okay. I won't tell him where I am. Or maybe my cousin Mario, at least? I mean, we grew up together. He has to be worried sick."

I am one thousand percent not the person she should ask these things to. Not because I wouldn't let her, I mean I wouldn't, but that's not the point. She was so far off base approaching me versus Ares it made me wonder if she already had and that was what was bothering him.

"No."

"No?"

"Why don't you tell me what's really going on?"

"I'm not lying."

"I didn't say you were, but someone like you doesn't let things like not talking to Daddy for a couple of days rattle her."

"Someone like me?"

I reached for her arm and nearly threw her on the bed. The fear in her eyes sparked something deep inside me that wanted out. I shook it off and moved to her. She had on another one of those little dresses Ares bought her and it rode up when she scrambled back from me toward the headboard.

"Are you scared of me, Valentina?" I asked as I crawled up the bed to where she was.

"No."

"Then why are you running?"

"I'm... I'm not."

I pulled the knife I kept on me out from behind my back and ran the blunt side of it up the soft skin of her leg. "I think I scare you la mia bella ragazza. I also think that beautiful little mind of yours could run circles around all of us, but you are hiding who you really are. That fear of us learning your desires is eating you up inside and we've only just begun."

She shivered at my words and the feeling of my blade. I caged her in with my body so she had nowhere to run to. She could feel the soft scratch of the cool metal against her skin after I flipped my blade. I used it to lift the dress she was wearing up to her hip, and she didn't dare stop me. Her breathing was heavy and her eyes had gone wide. The fear mixed with desire and the unknown and she was here for it. She was here for all of it.

"Is this what you need, my beautiful little girl? Do you need my blade to release the tension?"

Her head jerked as I ran it over the scars on her upper thigh. The other night she tried to hide her breasts from me but never had she covered the scars. They were thin lines of varying shades. Some old others newer, but all of them told the story of a girl who needed more than the world had given her.

"When did it start?"

"I was sixteen."

"The year you learned about Dante?"

"Yes."

"Did you cut yourself because of that?"

"No."

"What was it?"

"That was the first year my father locked me away. The first time I lost total control."

"Control is earned, not something given in this house."

"I understand that."

"Do you? Because you have all the right words, yet I found you in here unraveling at the seams. Do you want to cut yourself, Valentina?"

"No."

"Why not?"

"Because it's wrong."
"Would you rather I do it for you, then?"

CHAPTER THIRTEEN

VALENTINA

Nico was crazed. I laid as still as possible as his knife traced the scars on my legs. The scars I had forgotten about until recently. The same ones that tingled at the thought of doing it again. I wanted to do it. I had spent the last hour trying to come up with a way to cut myself again, but it didn't matter if I found something to do it or not. They would see the wound. That's the only thing that kept me from doing it. I didn't want to have to answer to Dante about it or see the look of pity in Ares' eyes. Now I was trapped between the headboard and a man who everyone, including his best friends, told me to be careful around and he was asking if I wanted him to do it for me.

"Valentina, I asked you a question," he said as the knife came up and he used the blade to lift my chin. "Would you like me to do it for you?"

I closed my eyes as the tears pooled. Nico would see right through my lies, so I did the only other thing I could think of at that moment. I told him the truth.

"Yes," I whispered. Cutting always provided me with the control I was so desperate for. I suffered from so much anxiety there was something calming about knowing if I opened my skin with a blade, I would bleed. It was a guarantee and one of the only ones I had in my life. Allowing Nico to do it was a whole other scenario I never would have thought I'd want. However, the second he asked the relief that ran through me and the wetness that dampened my panties couldn't be argued with.

He sat back on his heels and pulled me up to him. With one swift move, my dress was gone, and I sat there in nothing but a pair of pink lace panties and a matching bra that I'm sure Ares had picked out. His hand came to my chest and pushed me back onto the bed with more force than was necessary. Anywhere Nico touched me burned with desire. It was like that whenever he was close. Something inside of me recognized something deep within him and it was as if we would ignite if we let it go too far.

His blade was sharp and cool and unmistakably erotic. The danger that in a moment's time he could end me was lingering in the back of my mind and it should terrify me, make me push him away or run, but it did nothing of the sort. Nico was like a high you chased a million times over trying to reach the peak you had the first time he touched you. I couldn't look away from him. His eyes were dark, almost black, and suddenly I felt a snap and the cool air running over my breasts. He had cut right through my bra and never even bothered to look.

The thrill that ran through my body caused me to shiver, this time in need. I needed this. I needed him in a way Ares and Dante would never understand.

"So precious," he murmured as his blade ran alongside my breast, only to come up and slap my nipple with the flat edge of the blade. I yelped in surprise, but the sweet sting was quickly turned to pleasure as his mouth came down over it. Nico sucked and bit at me as I writhed beneath him. In the back of my mind I wondered, even worried, where the blade had gone, but I opened myself to him and wrapped my legs around his waist. He was still dressed in a soft pair of dress pants and a white dress shirt. I noticed when he came in, he was barefoot and his shirt was unbuttoned showing off his numerous tattoos. My mind drifted to the idea that maybe one day I could get my very own crown tattoo to match the ones each of them had on their middle finger.

Nico thrust his hips forward and I could feel how hard he was through his pants. It infuriated me he didn't just strip down and plunge himself inside of me. I was still sore from the night before, but he had worked me up into such a tizzy all was forgotten.

He pulled back and everything went dark. Nico's hand came over my eyes and I fought to pull away.

"Don't move," he growled out and then before I knew what was happening, I felt it. The knife pressed into my stomach and dragged its way across my midsection. But it didn't burn, it didn't sting like it was cutting me. At first, I wanted to scream but then I realized he hadn't actually stabbed me. I didn't know what to think. My eyes were still covered when my hands reached for my stomach, confirming what I already knew. There was no blood. Nothing but the faint feeling of relief mixed with a strange disappointment.

Disappointment? Was I really disappointed that he hadn't just filleted me open on the white comforter Ares had picked out? What the hell was wrong with me? I pulled my hands back and reached for him. Nico dragged his hand slowly away from my eyes and all I could see was his sadistic smile looking back at me.

"La mia bella ragazza, tell me, did you really believe I would kill you? Here, like this?"

"I... I don't know."

Nico moved to stand and pulled my body down the bed once he had. I was laying back with my legs dangling off the side and he leaned over me breathing in my scent like an animal ready to devour its prey. He stopped at my center and slid aside my panties, sticking a finger roughly into my core. He swirled it inside of me, then held it up for me to see it glisten in the light.

"You filthy little girl. Look at what mess you've made of those fancy little panties. Tell me Valentina, was it the knife or my cock that got you all riled up?"

"You."

"That wasn't an option."

"That's my answer. It's your knife and your cock. But in truth, it's the way you look at me. The way you want to break me, I can see it in your eyes, Nico, and it's fucking amazing," I said as I lifted my hands to my breasts, massaging them and pinching at my nipples while Nico stood licking his lips and watching my every move.

I didn't have to wait long for him to break. He threw his knife down on the bed next to me and flipped me over. The bed was high off the ground and I could just barely touch the floor. He yanked my panties from my body and I could hear him unbuckle his pants. When the zipper came down, I had only a second to brace myself before he impaled me with his cock. I screamed out at the intrusion. It burned and yet felt amazing at the same time. He laid the cool metal of the knife on my back and the weight of it grounded me in the moment. Nico still hadn't cut me, and the anticipation of when and how was coursing through my body as he pulled out and thrust in again, even harder than before.

"Oh, fuck!" I yelled as his movements became more and more intense. My whole body shook as he pounded into me, then his hand came up and gripped my hair in the same way Dante had the night before. He pulled hard and turned my head so I could see him out of the corner of my eye.

"Is this what you wanted, you little slut? Did your greedy little pussy need me to fuck it?"

"Yes. Please don't stop."

"Oh, I won't stop, pretty girl. That's Dante's game, not mine."

He let go of my hair and grunted as he held my hips, thrusting into me at a punishing pace. The thoughts of how much this was going to hurt later had gone and the only thing I could feel was Nico and his knife. Every time he thrust into me, it hit deeper and deeper until finally his hard cock found that one special place inside of me. I gasped at the feeling of it and cried in relief as my climax built. I gripped the bedding, trying to hold on as Nico's movements became more erratic. He was close and so was I. The way he was taking me was intoxicating and felt completely different from what I experienced last night.

My body shook as my orgasm crashed into me. I cried out Nico's name as my walls held him tight inside of me and the familiar wash of ecstasy came over me.

Nico wasn't done, though. My climax slowed, and he pulled himself from me quickly. My legs could barely hold my weight when he lifted me from the bed, but it didn't matter. He pushed me to my knees, and I looked up at him as he grabbed his cock and jerked himself off, grunting as the hot spurts of cum came down over my chest. I looked up at him in awe. I had never seen something so primal, so erotic in my life. He was watching over me when I opened my mouth and licked him clean.

"Very good, la mia bella ragazza. Such a good little slut."

I should be pissed off, aggravated with the fact that he continued to refer to me as both his beautiful little girl and a greedy slut, but I wasn't. I wanted it; I wanted more of it. My mind was fucked and at twenty-one years old I was getting to the point where I needed to just give in to it.

"I'm not done with you yet," he said as he put himself back together. Once he put himself away, he unbuttoned his dress shirt and threw it to the floor next to me. Then he reached for my hand and I stood. The feeling of his cum dripping down my body had me turning into a lust filled monster. I wanted more.

"Lay down."

Nico helped me to the bed and stood over me. He had his knife in his hand and a smile on his face. This time

I knew the instant he broke skin. The feeling of it was different than anything I had experienced before. He had cut along the top of my inner thigh, a place I knew held the oldest scars. He looked away from me and down at my leg.

"So beautiful," he said as the blade stopped and he lifted the knife to his mouth. I watched as he carefully licked the few droplets of blood from it and set it on the nightstand. His hand reached for where he had opened my skin and the sweet sting I loved so much combined with the heat of his oversized hand. He pinched at my skin and smiled wider as it bled more. Then, with the lightest of touch, his blood covered hand made its way up my body. I looked down and watched as he ran his fingers that were covered in my blood over his cum that was cool and beginning to dry on my skin. The sight was too much to behold. I moaned and closed my eyes, reaching between my legs to find myself still wet and now more sore than ever. None of it mattered though, I needed to come again. I slipped my finger into my folds and rubbed soft circles around my hardened clit as Nico sat on the edge of the bed. His hands never left my body. One was still playing in the mess of blood and cum on my breasts and the other had reached down over my hand that was pleasuring me. He didn't take the task over, but held his finger over mind as I continued my movements. It was as if he were trying to learn just how I liked it.

I didn't take long for things to escalate. I was so close, but I need more.

"Tell me again how dirty I am," I whispered to him as my eyes closed and I focused only on the movements of our joined hands.

"Dirty? You are fucking filthy," he said, "My filthy little whore who has made a mess of herself."

Nico pinched my nipple so hard I yelled out in pain. "Do you like that little whore? The pain mixed with the pleasure?"

"Yes."

"That greedy little pussy of yours didn't get enough last night or today. It needs another release even after you've been fucked."

"It does."

"Then come." He growled out as he leaned forward and I felt his teeth on my neck. The pain of his bite sent me over the edge. I couldn't hold back anymore. I didn't even want to. My body shook as my hips thrust upward and I saw stars as my orgasm hit me like a sledgehammer.

"Thank you," I whispered when I could finally find my voice.

Nico stood and left my room. I laid there covered in blood, cum and god knows what else, unable to move while my heart broke open at the sight of him leaving. The tears in my eyes were nothing compared to the hurt I felt deep inside of me. I lifted my hands to my face and finally gave into the emotional melt down I had been holding off for the last two days.

What had I done? Was I really nothing but a whore to him? Not only was I concerned about the decisions I was making, I was now bleeding everywhere, and Dante would certainly see the cut. My body shook as my mind broke apart, and all I could do was try my hardest to breathe. My chest hurt and the pain in my leg wasn't even helping. I couldn't believe he would just leave me here after all that we had just did. It just didn't feel right, but my mind couldn't seem to make heads or tails of it. Nico wasn't like the others, and maybe this was part of it. Maybe this was how things would be with him, and it was just something I needed to accept.

I pulled myself to a seated position and looked over at the nightstand. His knife was still sitting there, and I reached for it. I had just turned it over in my hand when I felt his presence. I was still crying, although not as hard. The tears wouldn't stop and I looked up to find him standing in the open doorway. That's when I realized he hadn't closed it behind him. If he left his knife and didn't close and lock the door, did he really leave? I couldn't trust my mind anymore.

"You left me."

"Only for a minute," he said, holding up a small first aid kit, "I needed to get supplies to clean you up."

He didn't try to come closer, and I didn't know what else to do. We sat there for what felt like an eternity. Nico's beast seemed to have calmed, but the fire in his eyes was still there.

"Are you okay?" he finally asked.

I shook my head as the tears picked back up again, "I don't think I am."

He came to me, climbed into the bed and pulled me to him. I was a mess and likely ruining not only the bedding but also his dress pants. He didn't seem to care about any of it.

"Shhh, mia bella ragazza." He held me tightly to him as he said, "I've got you. I would never leave you. I should have told you where I was going. This is my fault, not yours."

I have no idea how long we stayed like that. It could have been an eternity for all I knew. Eventually, the emotional turmoil of the last couple days and the adrenaline rush we had just experienced all came crashing down. My eyes closed and the last thoughts I had before I drifted off to sleep was how quickly I was falling for these men.

CHAPTER FOURTEEN

NICO

After my first night with Valentina, I promised myself she would never wake up without me. Luckily, Ares and Dante didn't seem to mind when I went crawling into bed every morning to fuck her slowly before her day began. Ares still hadn't brought her to his bed, and I was past the point of guessing what was going on with him. Dante's sleeping habits were shit, so when she didn't sleep with me, I would often find her tucked in his bed or hers after he was already awake for the day. It seemed we were finally getting a handle on the situation between the four of us. We had shared partners before, but never anything like this. Valentina was forever and I can be a selfish prick. I didn't want to rock the boat, but I also wanted time with her to myself nearly every day.

I stood in the doorway of her bedroom. We had all slept there, but it was late and I already got up to grab coffee and some breakfast for her. Watching my beautiful little girl sleep was an indulgence I'd never get used to. She was still finding her way between us all, and spent a lot of time on edge. It was moments like these, alone in the morning or late at night, that I learned more about who she really was.

I walked into the room and placed the food I brought for her on the nightstand. It could wait a little longer. I stripped out of my shorts and slid into bed behind her. My cock was more than ready for its morning treat and I pulled her to me, pressing myself into her backside.

"Mmmm... good morning." She mumbled as she pushed her ass back into my cock. I couldn't wait to get into that tight little hole of hers.

"I brought you breakfast."

"You brought me more than just breakfast."

"True."

I reached over her hip and slipped my fingers between her folds. Valentina opened herself up for me with ease, propping one leg over mine and shifting onto her back so she could look up at me. Those dark brown eyes of hers captivated my very soul when she looked up at me like this. Some days I wondered if it was nothing more than physical attraction, but then moments like this happen and I realize I am crazy about the woman in my arms.

"I missed you this morning." She whispered as I traced slow and gentle circles around her clit to tease her.

"I wasn't gone long, just enough time to get you food. I didn't think you would notice."

"Even while I sleep, I notice your absence." She said as I leaned forward and covered her mouth with my own.

My middle finger dipped into her core to find the sweet wetness I desired was already pooling there.

"My little slut is already so wet for me."

"Hmm... yes."

"Does this cunt need to come?"

"Yes, please."

I covered myself in her juices and I slid my fingers back up to her clit. She cried out as I moved from teasing to a full assault on her senses. Her hips shifted up into my hand as I moved from kissing her to biting the delicate skin of her neck. Her hand wrapped around my arm and she gripped me tightly as the first waves of her ready and waiting orgasm hit. Watching her come was the highlight of my day. Her body tensed as her lips parted. She looked me straight in the eye as she came and the need to be inside her was uncontrollable.

I shifted in bed, never missing a step while stroking her clit. She hadn't even fully come down from her high when I lifted her leg with my other hand and forced myself into her quivering cunt.

"Fuck." I grunted as she reached for me, pulling me to her by wrapping her arms around my back.

"More, please Nico. I want to come again."

"You never need to ask, my love."

I rocked into her body with more force than necessary. I couldn't control myself, not any longer. Every day wasn't enough, multiple times a day wasn't enough. I would never reach the point of enough when it came to my beautiful little girl.

"Yes! Yes, just like that!"

She cried out as I hit her g-spot with each thrust and before I knew it, the telltale sign of my own climax crept up my body.

"Now, Valentina. Come for me now." I growled as I emptied myself into her and she screamed out my name.

I fell on top of her, unable to hold myself up. There was no point in trying to hide how quickly she could get to me, how fast and hard I needed to flood her center every time I was inside of her. Valentina undid me.

"I'm going to get something to clean us up." I said as I pushed back up trying not to crush her under my weight.

"Didn't think ahead?" She teased with a small laugh.

"It's hard to think clearly when I'm standing over your sleeping body." I said, placing a small kiss on her nose before pulling out and heading into the bathroom.

"You know..." I heard her say from where I left her in bed, "I don't think you are the big scary Nico Marchesi everyone says you are. I think under that hard exterior you really are just the sweet man who makes me come every morning."

Her words filled me with hope and dread. There was still so much she didn't know about me, but I wasn't certain when the right time would be to tell her. If I could erase my past and all the trouble it has brought me, I would. I was living with a reputation I needed to maintain because without Valentina I was the manic beast people claimed I was. It was only when I was with her that I felt peace, so holding on to what we were building had now become my number one priority.

I cleaned myself up and brought a warm washcloth to take care of her. Once we settled back in bed, I placed the plate of food in front of her.

"Eat."

She picked up a piece of bacon and slipped it in between her lips. I had never wanted to be a piece of meat more than I did in that moment.

"Why do you go through all the trouble of feeding me every morning? You do realize we could go down and eat with the guys, right?"

"I like bringing you food. It's important that you take care of yourself. Ares and Dante's schedules are all fucked up, so it's easier for me to make sure you have breakfast. Ares takes care of lunch, and Dante makes sure he is here for dinner."

Her eyes went wide as I spoke.

"Did you not notice?"

"I guess I didn't. Did you all plan this?"

"Not really, it just sort of worked out that way. Why plan or change something that seems to work already?"

"Hm."

"Does it bother you?"

"No. I don't think so. It should, though, shouldn't it?"

"I don't think so, but I'm not you."

"I guess there are just so many things to consider being with all of you. I asked both Dante and Ares what to expect, and they don't seem to have any answers."

"Your need to plan everything is a form of control. Probably a way you deal with anxiety. None of us knows what the future will hold, but we all know you will be part of it."

"You sound like a shrink."

"I should, considering how many I've seen over the years."

"Did any of them help?"

"No."

"Maybe you just didn't find the right one."

"I don't think that's it. You have to believe in that stuff for it to work and I don't. At least, I don't believe in it for me."

"Why do you say that?"

"If it could help, then it would have by now. Ares and Dante spent a long time trying to help me or find me answers. I've had some pretty shit years and none of it worked."

She was quiet for a minute, thinking through what I said as she ate.

"Is there anything that makes it better for you? Or just easier?"

I smiled, "You."

The blush that rose up her cheeks was so damn adorable I wanted to throw her plate to the side and bury myself in her again.

"That's ridiculous."

"Think what you want, but it's the truth. It's not like I'm magically healed from my fucked up brain, but having you here, fucking your sweet little pussy every morning, holding you while you sleep at night… all of those moments help me feel almost normal."

The look she gave me was so intense it made me worry what she was going to say next. "Nico I—"

"Where the fuck are you two?" Ares shouted as he made his way down the hallway. "It's nearly ten."

"Shit." she muttered as she took her last bite of eggs and hopped out of bed to kiss Ares.

"Hmmm... very nice. I love a naked doll in the morning." he said as he pulled her into his arms then looked over at me. "Dante's waiting for you and he's getting pissed."

"Fucking hell." I got up and pulled my shorts on, then made my way to Valentina. She was still in Ares's arms as I leaned over to kiss her. "I'll be back later. I need to meet with Dante and run some errands."

"Okay."

I left them as my mind ran through every possible scenario of what she was about to say. I couldn't tell if it was something bad or good. My heart hoped she was about to tell me she loved me, but my mind squashed that thought as soon as it popped up. Valentina couldn't love someone like me, and she certainly couldn't have fallen for me this quickly. I went to my room and jumped in the shower. Today was going to be another long day of shit.

CHAPTER FIFTEEN

ARES

Time was moving too quickly for anyone's liking. It was the night of the Romano auction... or should I say, the Costa auction, and Valentina was growing impatient. She wanted answers and last night I almost broke and gave them to her. I had two guys working on her 'disappearance' and they had played their roles perfectly. Leo and Noah had only worked with us for a few years, but they were loyal and hard workers. They were the kind of men everyone needed on their payroll. They were also nearly identical twins, so when I needed them to be two people they could, but when I needed them to be one person, they could do that too. A trick they had perfected over the years and one that always amazed even me.

They did not cancel the auction, much to our dismay. Costa had been trying to keep it all together, but the results disappointed a ton of families. The quality of the women wasn't what it had been in the past, and you could hear the creeps mumbling their annoyance. I sat next to Dante in the front row and my skin crawled as they paraded young girls on stage who had been painted in more makeup than they needed. Most had tears streaking their faces, which just added to the unrest in the client base. Trafficking was not a business we got into and it never would be. Tonight would be the last auction. We would see to that in the same way we had recovered thirteen of the fifteen women they sold the last time.

"I don't know how much more I can take."

"Of what? The girls or Valentina?"

I let out a small laugh. "Both actually."

"You've been distancing yourself from her."

"She asks too many questions when we are alone."

"Like what?"

"About her father, about what happened the night we took her. The Costas, our future. All of it. I can't keep lying to her, Dante."

We sat in silence as they brought out yet another girl. At one point, I had actually considered just buying them all so I could let them go, but that would have ruined our plan. Nico was home alone with Valentina which meant by the time we made it back she'd be fucked, cut and sleeping. The night Dante found out what Nico had done to her, he lost his shit. It had been years since I had seen him that angry with him, but it couldn't be helped. I let them scream and beat the fuck out of each other in the main house while I laid in bed and held Valentina as she cried.

I told her too much about us that night. In an effort to calm her down, I explained how common it used to be for the two of them to fight. I told her how Dante wasn't mad at her or even about what happened, but it was that Nico didn't honor his request.

It wasn't until Nico came to bed and pulled her to him that she relaxed. I stayed with them that night and a few others, but I hadn't pressed things with Valentina. I wanted her to know the truth, and if I fucked her the way I wanted to, I knew I would tell her anything she ever asked of me. She was a smart girl and strong as hell, but she'd had everything stripped away from her and was on unsteady ground. Nico kept pushing her, and Dante was getting impatient. He had held off on everything he wanted from her because Nico was out of control. The problem was that Valentina didn't believe him to be. She insisted he was everything she wanted and kept getting angry with Dante for trying to control their relationship. The dynamic between us all was different this time. We were in this for the long haul, not just some girl we shared for a few nights. Adjusting to this new way of life was harder than any of us had expected.

Leo came back with news that a local bar back was telling everyone he had seen Valentina in the bar a few nights ago. Nico didn't say a word, but got up and left the house. Dante was in bed with Valentina, so I had to go after him. By the time I got there, the guy was already dead. Beaten to death behind the bar while he was closing up for the night.

Cleaning up Nico's messes was a full-time job that I didn't have time for, so me and him were at odds too.

"I want to take her to the shop."

"No."

"She needs to get out of the house."

"No, she doesn't. She has everything she needs there."

"Letting her out of her room wasn't setting her free, Dante. She needs more than that."

Dante didn't say a word, so I left it alone. This situation was taxing on all of us, but I heard him pacing night after night. He only slept the nights Valentina was with him, otherwise he would just move from the office to his bedroom all night long working and stressing out over the shit storm we were dealing with.

"When we are done with the Costas you can take her. I don't want anyone knowing she's alive."

The auction ended and the second we stood, people wishing to speak with Dante and I surrounded us. Not many families ran like the Corsettis but the equal balance between the three of us allowed us all to excel in areas we were best. It always kept some of the pressure off Dante, but still allowed for the same message.

"Ares, so good to see you." The slithering voice of Elisabetta made my entire body tense. I saw her sitting down when we walked in and said a silent prayer that she wouldn't bother me tonight. I wasn't lucky though and now her nasty long blood-red nails were moving their way down the lapel of my suit jacket.

I reached for her hand and pulled it away, "Elisabetta, what a surprise. I wouldn't take this as your typical crowd."

"Daddy is here tonight to buy a present for Fredric and I didn't want to miss out on all the fun. I see you didn't buy a toy tonight. Did nothing strike your fancy?"

"Will you excuse me? I have a call to make."

I stepped aside and pulled my phone from my coat pocket, leaving the nosey tramp to herself. Looking over,

I caught the evil eye of her father. For years he had tried to get me to agree to marry his daughter and for years I had politely declined. If it didn't stop, then I'd have to be more forceful than planned. Nico answered on the second ring but it wasn't his voice I heard; it was Valentina's.

"Harder, yes! More!" the unmistakable sound of him fucking her was loud and clear.

"Like that little whore? Shout for me. Tell me how bad you want my cock."

"I need it, Nico, please," she whined, and I nearly came in my pants like a schoolboy at the sound of it all.

"Such a slut, scream. Let Ares hear how good you feel."

He must have moved the phone because her breathing was more distinct and her voice was clear.

"Oh fuck, Ares.... I need you. Come home. Please," she whined as Nico's grunts became louder and her cries became more frequent.

I watched Dante approach, with a smile on my face.

"What are you doing?"

"Listening to La mia piccola bambola, get fucked," I handed him the phone, and he turned away from the crowd as the look of shock came over his face.

"Ragazzina," he said in a low voice that sounded like something came from deep within him, "What are you doing?"

I couldn't hear her respond, but his was clear as day. "I will punish you tonight for teasing Ares. Do you understand me?"

He smiled slightly and handed the phone back to me. She was crying out her release right as the phone went dead. Nico, the asshole, cut her off at my favorite part.

"Can we go home now?"

"No. We have one thing left to take care of."

"What is that?"

"Valentina's cousin just arrived."

I looked to the door and saw a short, thin man with slicked back black hair enter. Valentina's cousin Mario was technically the only surviving heir to the Romano family business. However, everything was left to Valentina, not him, which only made him frustrated over the red tape he was trying to work through. Sure, they were friends when they were kids, but there was no sign that they were still close. Her being alive would only complicate matters for him and his new business plans. He was yet another thing we needed to deal with in order to move on with our lives. Between shutting down this trafficking mess, Angelo Costa, and now Mario Romano it felt like we would never be free of the bullshit.

"Come on, let's get this over with."

The man reached for Dante's hand first. "Don Corsetti, it's always good to see you."

"Mario, I want to wish you our condolences for your recent loss."

"Thank you, sir."

He turned in my direction with an outstretched hand and I didn't bother with the niceties Dante had already laid out. This guy gave me a weird feeling. He always had, but the idea of him only fucked with me more now that we had Valentina. I remember him running around after us as a snot-nosed kid when we were younger and now here he stood dressed in a suit pretending to be something he's not.

"I'm afraid you missed the auction."

"Yes, I had planned to be here earlier, but something came up. I still came in hopes I would see all of you. Is Nico here?"

"No. He's attending to other business tonight."

"Strange, isn't it? It's rare the three of you are separated, yet lately people say they only ever see two of the kings together at once."

"Do you have something you want, Mario?"

"There are rumors of my cousin circulating the city. That she's alive and well, but in hiding. As you can imagine, this is wonderful news for our family, but I have to wonder why the men you have working on finding her keep coming up empty."

"You're dancing pretty close to the line, Mario. I'd take a step back and shut the fuck up if I were you," I said as I stepped in front of Dante.

Mario took two steps back. "You misunderstand me. Really, I'm very grateful to Angelo for reaching out to you all, but I'm still in mourning. Maybe my words weren't the best choice."

Dante stepped around me and then headed for the door. I took his lead and walked away. There was no need to stay here and deal with this man's shit. Tonight, the focus was the auction. Next would be Angelo. Mario Romano wasn't on our list of top priorities right now.

My phone rang as we stepped outside to meet our driver at the valet.

"My men are in position," Jason Calvano said before I even said hello, "I need to know that the timing is correct because I have a half a mile of SUV's holding warrants for everything from RICO charges to murder. They are hungry for the men inside that building."

"Timing is fine. We are leaving now."

I ended the call and got into the car as it pulled up.

"Are they ready?" Dante asked as soon as the door closed.

"They are moving in now."

The car rounded the bend, heading to the expressway, and as soon as we passed the lead vehicle, red and blue lights lit up the sky. Jason wasn't lying. There had to have been fifty SUVs starting their engines and working their way to the warehouse the auction had just taken place. Over the years, we had learned that sometimes it was just easier to turn over the assholes than it was to kill them all.

"Looks like a busy night for the feds," I said with a laugh.

"Sure does. But it's one less thing that we need to deal with."

"And it builds more trust between us and the firm."

Calvano Security was the largest private security firm in the city, and they weren't fans of bribes. Every once in a while, we would trade. Tonight was one of those nights. We hand over a human trafficking ring and they turn a blind eye when we need them to. A win-win for all involved.

When we got back to the house, it was eerily quiet. I grabbed a drink before heading back to the bedrooms and when I arrived, I found Valentina in Dante's room with Nico. Dante was undressing as he approached her, but that wasn't what was surprising. What surprised me was where she was, not who she was with. I stepped inside to find her tied to a black leather and wood spanking bench. One Dante had ordered months ago, but kept hidden until now. Her ass was high in the air and she had a gag in her mouth. Nico had held nothing back tonight. He had fucked her and prepped her for her punishment. I looked over at him to see he was sitting in a chair with a shit-eating grin on his face, then I turned my attention back to the sweet little ass that was about to be destroyed.

CHAPTER SIXTEEN

DANTE

Tonight was it. One of those moments you felt like you've been waiting for your entire life. I walked into the house to silence, which always made me uneasy. Nico and Valentina were growing closer by the day and I did my best to keep my distance, allowing them to work out their own relationship while Ares seemed to punish himself by staying away. Things were complicated at the house, and he was right, she was growing uneasy about being stuck here. Tonight was a big night for us. Although we weren't the ones handling everything, the partnership with Calvano Security allowed me to keep my hands clean and still bring down Angelo Costa.

Now that the first step was completed, we could reintroduce her to the world. Her cousin Mario was still an issue, but nothing we couldn't handle with a bullet if needed. Her behavior was exceptionally good considering her circumstances, so it was only now that I would have the chance to introduce her to my personal form of play. I still struggled with trusting her willingness to accept us as who we were, but without any outside influence, it was only us and the bond we were creating. One that would last a lifetime.

I approached the bench without any toys. I wanted my hand on her flesh tonight. The bench was custom made and delivered a few months back. I hadn't used it with anyone else. None of the toys we had for Valentina had been. Everything was new and purchased specifically for her.

"Ragazzina, you have misbehaved today." I ran my fingers over her plump ass and down her back, feeling her body tremble beneath my touch. "You allowed Ares and I to be teased by the sounds of your pleasure when we were too far to do anything about it. That is not good behavior at all. In fact, I'm certain it's some of the worst behavior you have displayed since you've joined us."

I bent down and lifted her chin to look her in the eyes. Her hair was down and covering her face. I wanted to see it; see everything I was doing to her tonight.

"Get me a hair tie." I said, looking over at Ares. While he got up to gather something, I pulled her hair back and carefully braided it so it would stay in place. Valentina smiled as I did it and closed her eyes as if she were the happiest little girl in the whole world. The look nearly undid me. When Ares returned, I secured the end and pulled the gag out of her mouth.

"Look at me, Ragazzina. Do you remember your pain scale?"

"Yes, sir."

"When I ask where you are, you must be honest. I will not forgive you if you lie to me. Only a 5 will stop what is about to happen to you."

"I understand, sir."

My cock twitched every time she acknowledged who I was to her. I was her sir, and only hers. The ownership of something so precious was the greatest gift. Tonight she would learn what her sir was truly capable of.

I walked to the cabinet in the corner of my room and opened it. A smile came over me as I ran my hands over each of the items I had gathered to please my little girl with.

"Nico, get a mirror. I want her to see her face as she cries out in pain."

Without bothering to look back, I picked up a plug and a bullet that I'd tease her with. Her punishment would come in many ways, impact being only one of them.

I placed the toys down on the side of the bed as Nico came back in with a large mirror from his bedroom. He placed it in front of Valentina and I watched as she lifted her chin to see herself. A blush came over her cheeks and I knew she was just as pleased with the state of things as I was.

"Open your legs for me. Let me see your pussy." Nico had restrained her arms but not her legs. I wanted her wide open as I filled her tonight.

Valentina squirmed as I ran my finger through her folds and dipped into her center. She was already so wet that when I removed my finger and replaced it with the toy, it slid in easily as she moaned.

"You will not come. If you do, your punishment will increase. Do you understand?"

"Yes, sir," she whined but nodded her head slightly to confirm.

"Ares will control what happens between your legs while I deliver your spankings," I said as I handed the small remote to him.

As soon as I turned back to her, he flipped the switch. Valentina's body thrust forward and she let out a cry and then, just as quickly as he turned it on, he stopped it. I watched as she took in a couple of deep breaths, then her head lifted and she looked at me in the mirror.

"Tell me, little girl, what's your number?"

"A one. I'm ready."

"Do you understand tonight's rules?"

"I do."

"Very good."

Without warning, I reached back and slapped her ass with less force than I would have liked. It still provided the delicious sting in my palm and the intended pain response from my little one. She groaned and leaned back, perking her plump behind up, looking for more.

"Did you like that, little girl?"

"Yes, sir."

"That's one." I pulled my hand back and right before I made contact, I could hear the soft buzz of the vibrator and Valentina's scream.

"Two."

She was moaning and pulling against her restraints, but she held on tight and waited for the next one.

"Three. Four." The next two peppered her ass a bit harder than the others. Her hips thrust forward and her groans grew heavy.

"Do Not Come."

"Yes... sir," she ground out between clenched teeth.

"Five. Six." Her breathing had increased, and she was biting her lower lip so hard I wouldn't be surprised if she drew blood.

"Don't do it, little girl. Don't let go." I slapped her again, twice more, but lower on the back of her thighs and right as her mouth dropped open, Ares stopped the toy.

"Fuck!" she yelled and then her eyes went wide. Her gaze darted up at me in the mirror and she looked as if she were terrified. I felt Nico move behind me. He fed off fear and hers was radiating throughout the room. She had fucked up, and she knew it. I stood watching as he rounded on her.

"Should I give you something to keep you quiet?" he said as he jerked his cock in her direction.

Valentina didn't respond, but looked back at me. I nodded in Nico's direction as he shoved his cock into her mouth. The sound of her choking combined with how gorgeous she looked was enough to undo me. Nico grabbed her braid and began fucking her mouth while I continued with her punishment.

Ares continued to torture her with the pulsing of the toy. Her ass was red and beginning to welt. I looked down at my hand. It had gone numb somewhere between strikes eleven and twelve. I stepped back, admiring our girl. She was perfection. While Nico kept her busy, I stepped aside and grabbed the lube from my nightstand. After coating first my finger, then the plug, I went to her and started the next part of her training. If she was going to take all of us, then it was going to take some work not to hurt her.

Valentina was groaning and choking as the tears ran down her face. Nico's grunts grew louder, and I knew he was close.

I pinched one of the red spots on her backside and she cried out, making eye contact with me again in the mirror.

"You will not come," I said as my finger pressed on her tight hole. She couldn't speak, couldn't move. All she could do was take what I was giving her. I plunged my finger deeper, stretching and prodding at her until she relaxed under my touch. When she did, I reached for the plug, replacing my finger with the smooth silicon point. I stepped back with the second remote in my hand right as Nico was about to lose it.

"Now, Valentina," I flipped the switch at the same time Ares did. The orgasm that shook her body was hard and fast. She had been edging for too long. Her body was ready, but her mind had no idea what had happened. Nico emptied himself into her mouth and, rather than taking the time to lick him clean when he pulled out, she grit her teeth and closed her eyes, letting out a guttural moan that nearly made me come. She was a vocal little girl and the sounds she made when she came were enough to undo all my control.

I turned off the plug and Ares followed suit. Nico leaned forward and placed a gentle kiss on her lips that she hadn't even registered before he stepped away. I pulled the toys from her ass and her cunt faster than I should have and quickly undid her restraints. I needed to be inside of her now.

When I had her free, I picked her up and moved her to my bed. The guys had left, but it didn't matter. I needed her tonight, and I needed her to myself. I sat on the bed and pulled her limp body over mine. She collapsed onto my chest and for a minute, I just clung to her. I never did things like that with a woman. I never had a desire to. Maybe it was because I had known for years she would be my wife, or maybe there was just something different about Valentina Romano, but the desire to hold her, protect her and care for her was a whole new thing for me.

She was straddling me with her wet folds enveloped my cock. After sometime she held me close and lifted her hips slightly as she ground herself onto my hard shaft. I looked down and her eyes were closed, but a soft smile had come across her face as she continued to use me for the pressure and friction she desired.

"Does your cunt need to be filled, Ragazzina?"

"Hmmmm.... yes sir."

I lifted her slightly and aligned myself with her entrance. She pressed up on my chest as I lowered her onto me. I felt like I was going to explode as she moved slowly, rocking her hips forward and back as she rode my cock.

"You're such a good little girl when you want to be. You did very well tonight, little one." She preened at my words and an uncomfortable thump in my chest made me once again question what this woman was doing to me.

She stared into my eyes as if she could see something deep within my soul and I thrust upward, fucking her from below. It didn't take long for her climax to take over. It had only been a couple of weeks, but given our situation, we spent more time fucking than we did anything else.

I knew her body in ways I hadn't known anyone's and I wouldn't trade it for a thing.

"Sir, can I... please, can I come?"

"Impatient?"

"I don't think I can stop it. I'm so close... I just need... I need..."

"Tell me, tell me what I can give you."

"Pain."

I lifted my hand and delivered two harsh and painful slaps to her backside. Her center clenched down on my dick like a vice grip and she moaned out a chorus of joy as I emptied myself into her sweet center. Nothing in this world could ever compare to Valentina.

After I bathed and massaged ointment into her backside, I dressed her and pulled her back onto me in the bed. The weight of her body was comforting and the soft sighs she let out were like music to my ears.

"Dante?"

"Yes, love."

"Will it always be like this?"

"It will."

"Okay."

"Is there something you want to change?"

"Between me and you, or all of us?"

"Me and you."

"No, we are perfect."

"Then what about all of us?"

"Sometimes at night I wonder what the future would really look like. I had these ideas in my head for so long, but now that I'm here, things are so different. I don't see how my father will ever accept all of you. And who would I marry? Would we all have children? Am I allowed to work? I know I just got here, but I have so many questions."

I rubbed slow circles into her back as I answered her. "Tomorrow we will all meet. There are things you have asked about and it's time you learned the truth about everything that has happened. As for our future together, I don't have all of those answers yet. Our only focus has been on getting you here. Now that you are, we will need to work out the logistics of everything. One thing I can tell you now is that you are ours and that will never change. I protect many people in this city and employ many more. You, my little girl, are more important than any of them. You will want for nothing. You will be treated as a queen, and you will stand by our side as we continue to control the business my family built years ago."

She took a deep breath but said nothing. I held her like that for longer than I would admit to Ares or Nico. Eventually, her breathing evened out and slowed as she fell asleep in my arms. Tomorrow was a day I had been dreading since we took her. She continued to refer to her father as if he were still alive and none of us had corrected her. He was an evil man and yet still he was her father. She had prepared herself for me, planned to be with me, but in the end, she never would have imagined the amount of men we killed to get to her. If she ran out on me now, I wasn't sure if I could make it out alive.

CHAPTER SEVENTEEN

ARES

Last night was intense, and this morning wasn't much better. I drank myself into a stupor just to fall asleep, and I was cursing the decision as I dragged my ass down to the kitchen. Nico was there, sitting at the table, looking miserable as usual. He had a cup of coffee in front of him, but it didn't look like he had taken a sip.

"Have they been down yet?"

"Dante's in his office. She wasn't awake when I saw him."

"What did he have to say?"

"That today would still go as planned. It's time she knows and we will deal with the repercussions as they come."

"And you're okay with that?"

"No."

I nodded and moved toward the espresso machine and made myself one. Not knowing how today would go, we scaled back staffing. If Valentina was going to fall apart, then we needed to focus on her. Not what others would see. After quick consideration, I topped it with grappa and sat down.

"She could leave us, you know."

"No, she can't. Where would she go?"

"Probably to that asshole cousin of hers."

"I'll kill him."

"We can't force her to stay."

"We can, and I will. Just so we are clear, your soft little heart will not fuck this up for us. Valentina belongs here, she belongs to us, and I'll chain her to the fucking wall if she tries to run."

I shook my head. Clearly, Nico wasn't in a rational state of mind. It was tension and fear and everything we didn't want it to be, but it was the truth. She could leave us, maybe not for her father's death, but the night we went for her, we essentially stripped away everything she had ever known. The house she grew up in, the staff that cared for her, the businesses her family ran. It was all gone now. Destroyed by The Dark Kings in a manner that only we were capable of.

"Hey."

I looked up at the sound of her voice. She was standing in the doorway to the kitchen, but wasn't making a move to come in. Every morning, our cook would prepare breakfast and leave it for us. I had found Valentina down here on more than one occasion chatting with the old man, so it's not like she had any need to be timid. I looked over at Nico, whose expression left nothing to the imagination. He was pissed the fuck off and shooting daggers in her direction. The poor girl hadn't even done anything yet, but I knew Nico better than most. He had already decided that she would try to leave and he was mad about it.

I stood and went to her, placing a soft kiss on her forehead and ushering her to the table. "Come and eat."

Her gaze shifted to Nico. "I'm not really hungry yet. Maybe just a coffee?"

"Sure. Sit and I'll get it for you."

I got to preparing her coffee as she liked. Nico's gaze hadn't left her and she couldn't seem to make eye contact with him. Considering he was the first one to stick his dick in her every morning, she had to have known something was up. It didn't matter whose bed she ended up in for the night, she always woke up with Nico. His need for her differed from ours. Hell, I hadn't even had her sleep in my bed yet, let alone fuck her. It'd been driving me insane, but she wouldn't stop asking me things I couldn't tell her. Avoiding alone time with her was the only way I had survived. I placed a cup of coffee down in front of her and took a seat.

"Is Dante here?"

"Yes, he's in the office waiting for us."

"Is that why Nico is mad at me?"

I looked up at my brother, annoyed that he was making her feel like shit, and all he did was shake his head and leave the room.

"He's not mad at you, La mia piccola bambola. He's just Nico."

"But he didn't come see me this morning and I can tell there is something wrong with him."

"We have a lot to discuss today. I think it just has everyone a little on edge." I picked up my cup and threw back what was left of it. Valentina reached for it and turned her nose up when she sniffed the liquor.

"He's not the only one upset this morning, is he?"

I stood and put my cup in the sink. "Come, bring your coffee. Let's get this over with."

We walked hand in hand to the office. Dante was sitting behind his desk with his head hidden behind his computer screen. Nico hadn't really made much of an effort to even pretend he was working. Instead, he had shoved everything aside. And appeared to be carving something into the wood of the desk. A desk I specially ordered for him from India when we set the office up. My love for antiques, rich artwork and all the luxuries of the world were lost on the Neanderthal I called my brother.

"Let's get this over with. I think we're all ready to just put this part behind us," I added as I took a seat at my desk.

Dante looked up but didn't smile as he usually did when he saw her. Instead, he reached a hand out and she went to him. He pulled her onto his lap and flush to his chest. I watched as he ran his fingers through her hair.

"Ragazzina, you will learn things this morning about us that you may not want to forgive. That's okay. You don't need to forgive us. But you do need to understand what happened and why. Today you will get a glimpse into what The Dark Kings really are about. The truth between the lines and the truth behind the rumors. Your family prepared you to come to me and you heard stories about who we were as a child. But it's not the same unless you hear it from us. You decided to stay here, to keep us as we are, and I will hold you to that. You will not run from me. Do you understand?"

Even as he held her, I could see how he revered her. She meant so much to him, and it had only been a short moment in time. Valentina closed her eyes and lifted her lips to his. As his mouth came down to meet hers, passion ignited between the two of them. He loved her. He may not know it yet, but he did. Nico's anger, combined with Dante's love for her, was sometimes too much to bear. I wanted that same fire to roar to life between us. But in trying to protect Valentina from our world, I had created a wedge between us instead. The more I thought about it, the more ridiculous it seemed. She knew what we were like. Her father wasn't much different. He was worse, actually. Not just a murderer to protect his family, but a human trafficker that sold young girls to the highest bidder. The list of terrible deeds goes on. Many would even venture to say Michael Romano and his family had no morals. Where the Corsettis had many they lived by.

"I understand."

"Ares, can you pull everything up?"

This was it. This was the moment I had been dreading. I hacked into their computer system and pulled every security camera's footage I could get my hands on from the night we were there. Not only to erase any trace of us. But to keep a record of what had happened, something that we could show her so that she could understand what she was getting into. I had watched the tapes repeatedly and every time, no matter which way I looked at them, all I could see were three crazed men murdering and torturing other humans to get to the woman they loved. A woman they loved, but they had never even had. None of it made any sense, but it was the way we lived. It was the way of our world and I only could hope and pray that Valentina would understand why we did what we did.

"Have a seat in one of the chairs," Dante said, pointing at a chair in front of his desk.

There was a large monitor on one wall that we used for videoconferencing. I launched the recording from the beginning. Us parking in the driveway, and walking in the front door as if we had done so a million times before. The guard shack was easy to get through. The men there were sleepy, not attentive, and not willing to risk their own lives to protect the family they were hired to guard.

"What is this?" Valentina interrupted as soon as it started.

I didn't bother stopping it or answering, I just trusted Dante would deal with the questions now.

"This is the night we took you."

She couldn't pull her eyes from the television. I watched as silent tears ran down her face. She didn't yell or scream; she didn't throw a fit, but she just sat there and watched as we murdered every person who she knew. When the footage clicked over to her father's office. She shook her head slightly, then began rocking back and forth. I wanted to go to her, to hold her and help her understand, but I was afraid she would push me away.

"No, no, no," she whispered to herself.

I had turned the audio down. There was no reason for her to have to listen to it all as well. We watched as an exchange happened between Dante and her father. It was short, and it ended with Dante lifting his gun and placing a bullet right between his eyes. I looked over at him. He couldn't pull his eyes from her, and she couldn't pull her eyes off the monitor. Nico looked as if he were dying inside. He knew what was coming next. We all did. We had quite a few heated conversations about this part of the tape, and Dante and I agreed she needed to see it.

There was a bit of dead air and then Valentina began counting quietly. One, two, three, four, five, six. Then again, one, two, three, four, five, six. My heart was breaking for my little doll. Sure, her father meant something to her, but the only person who she spoke highly of, the only person she talked about often, was the cook that Nico had brutally murdered that night.

Luckily, from the view of the camera, you couldn't see what was happening behind the counter. But what you could see was enough. Nico's face was one of rage. He was a complete animal at that moment. I had lost count of how many strikes he took, how many kicks he gave, how many punches he delivered. The men he had killed just to get to that point were numerous, but it was this murder, this person who meant so much to her, that broke her. I watched as Valentina fell forward onto the floor. She was on her knees, wringing her hands in front of her as she screamed and cried. She was mourning the death of her only friend. Probably the only person who ever cared for her. It was a response you would have expected to see from someone who watched their father die, but that man meant nothing to her compared to the woman behind the counter.

The man Dante killed tortured her, locked her away, and he used her as a puzzle piece. He shifted her around until he found the place she was most valuable, and Valentina knew that. She was nothing but a commodity to that man, but to the woman who taught her to cook, the woman who snuck her treats at night. She was the one that would hurt more than anything. I pressed stop and turned the video off. She had seen enough. I couldn't go on watching her break apart any longer.

The most she saw from me and Dante were a couple of gunshots to the heads of hired men and, of course, her father. I was the one who took out her father's current wife. I'm not even sure what her name was, honestly, and I don't think that mattered to Valentina at all. But what she saw in the end, that's what we all had to worry about. I didn't go to her. Neither did Nico nor Dante. We sat there for a very long time as she screamed and cried. And then suddenly she stood. And she turned on us.

"How could you? With everything that you knew about me, everything that you knew about my father and my family. It just doesn't make any sense. You didn't have to kill them all. They didn't have to all die!"

"They did, Ragazzina, and you will not question our decisions."

"Question your decisions? Question your decisions? Are you kidding me right now?! You came for me in the middle of the night after years of planning and tracking me down and you want me to believe that the only way to get me was to go into my family home and murder every person who had ever come in contact with me?"

"A message needed to be sent."

"So you used my life to send a message. Who was it for? There's no one left."

"That's not true," I interrupted, "Mario was not at the estate. He is alive and looking for you. Angelo Costa reached out to him immediately, and they worked to find an investigator to look into the incident at your home. Since your body was not recovered, they had a hard time believing you died."

"Died? What do you mean, recovered?"

"Your family's estate was burned to the ground that night. Dante told you there was nothing to go back to, and he meant it."

Valentina's jaw dropped. The rage was still clear in her eyes as she looked at the three of us. Well, the two of us. She glanced over at Nico, but quickly looked away. It almost seemed as if it was too painful for her to look at him. She never wanted to believe what we told her about him, not even the things he warned her about himself, but now she just watched murder her only friend and it was evident she understood it all now.

"I want to see him."

"No." Dante responded before I could say another word.

"Why not? It's obvious I'm not dead. He's going to figure it out sooner or later. Why delay the inevitable?"

"We had other loose ends that needed to be tied up before we could announce that you were with us."

"Like what?"

"Your father's business with Angelo Costa needed to end."

"His business? What business? He has a bunch of businesses."

"No, Valentina, he had a bunch of businesses. One of which was very much against the treaty in our area. One that was very much against anything he had ever been allowed to do in the past. When Dante denied his partnership, he went to Angelo. They have been selling women for almost two years now and last night, we ended that too."

"You killed Angelo Costa?"

"No. He's still alive. But he can't get you anymore."

"What have you been doing for the two weeks while I've been here? I feel like such a fool. Here I was falling in love with the three of you, spending my days wondering what time you'd come for me, fucking you all night long just to find out that while all that was happening you were.... I don't even know what you were doing. None of this makes any sense. There are meetings and negotiations and trades that happen between families. I know that much. I was always taught everyone has a price tag."

"When your father began the auctions and Angelo joined him, I warned them that if they did not stop, I would end it. I don't go back on my word."

"Then stop the auctions. I'm not for keeping them running. It's a disgusting thing to do. Where is Angelo?"

"Why do you fucking care?" Nico's voice cut in, "Really Valentina, what makes those people so important to you?"

"I didn't say they were important to me. I just am trying to understand what the fuck I've gotten myself into."

"But you didn't get yourself into anything, did you, little girl?" The snarl that came out of Nico as he added Dante's pet name for her wasn't missed. "Like you said, you were a piece of a puzzle. A piece that your father had put with us and then he took it away. He moved you to the Costas because that's where you were valuable to him. But he didn't get to do that. That's not how things work."

I stood and put an arm out in Nico's direction, as he went to move towards her. I didn't think he'd hurt her. But I also didn't think she wanted to be touched by any of us right now.

"There's more."

"Of course there is."

"Your cousin appears to be making movements. He's doing things he shouldn't be doing," I said, "You are the rightful heir of the Roman estate. I emptied all of your father's accounts and shut the businesses down. I transferred all of the assets into a holding company for you. Mario has no idea. He claims he's looking for you. Because of how close the two of you were and how important you are to the family. But he's made multiple attempts at different financial institutions to get information on the Romano family accounts."

"How do you know that? How do you know any of this? I don't think you've ever told me what your role is in this whole thing. Other than stealing priceless pieces of art just because you like them, I have no idea who you are or what you do."

Her words were truthful, but they still hurt.

"I find things. I find people and then I take the things and people as I need to. All you need to know is that I protect the Corsetti family. Each of us has a role that we play here. There's no need to pretend like you don't understand. I've been watching you, La mia piccola bambola. You are smarter than you appear. And you are likely more manipulative than you would ever admit. Most people would be terrified of us, but not you.. not even a little bit. The strength and resilience that you've shown as you grew up in that shit storm of a fucking disaster made you into who you are today. Much in the same way each of our own childhoods made us into who we are."

She looked away from me and wouldn't say anything else. Dante was quiet and just watching everything unfold. Nico picked up his knife and shoved it into the wooden desk. The noise made her jump and she turned to see him as he stood looking straight at her.

"What is it going to be, Valentina? Are you going to run from me now? Because I should warn you, I'm very good at catching my prey."

Her breathing increased. And her pupils dilated. Whatever was happening between her and Nico was something I would never understand. It was like they were two broken souls, just ready to tear each other apart. For Dante, she brought calm; she brought sanity. For Nico, she brought chaos, and for me, she brought home. She was home. She was my home. And it would kill me if she left.

CHAPTER EIGHTEEN

VALENTINA

It had been over a week, and I was still sick to my stomach every time I thought of the video that Ares had shown me. I was finally rationalizing what I had seen in my mind, but it was hard. I just kept telling myself repeatedly that I knew who they were. I knew what I was getting into and I knew why I was promised to them. But it didn't help. I was so angry at first, and then so devastatingly sad. The night I cried for my father was shocking to me. I didn't think I had any tears left for a man who had nearly destroyed me. He had essentially sold me from one family to the next until he got what he felt he deserved, but still I laid there in bed and I remembered the nights when I was a little girl and he'd come home from meetings all day. I'd go into his office and sit on the floor next to his desk. He'd let me play with my toys while he talked on the phone. No, it wasn't like a typical childhood. There was no throwing a ball around in the yard or him teaching me how to ride a bike. But those nights that I'd sat in his office seemed like the only chance I ever got to get to know who he was. My mother had died shortly after I was born. Which left me with no one but him. We had extended family, cousins and uncles that I barely knew, so at the end of the day he really was the only person I had in my life.

It was the death of Madeline that hurt the most. Nico had essentially slaughtered the woman on the floor of my kitchen. It was in that same kitchen that she taught me how to cook and cared for my scraped knees. She was the only woman who ever cared for me and I knew she had lived a good and long life, but she never, ever would have deserved what she was given. The stories of Nico butchering and murdering people were never lost on me. I always knew what he was capable of, but I never had expected to see it. He was terrifying. A monster that was uncontrollable in that moment. Even after seeing it, my heart still hurt for the man. There was something deep and tortured within him, and I still hadn't learned what it was. To be honest, it scared me to ask. Someday I would work up the courage and if I didn't, I trusted he would tell me. I don't know why I believed that as much as I did, but there was no convincing me otherwise.

I hadn't spoken to him or Dante. Ares came to me after two days of hiding away in my room. It was the first time I voluntarily stayed put. The risk of running into both of them was too much. It's not like Ares was any more innocent than they were, but Dante killed my father and Nico killed the only person who I ever loved. Ares didn't touch me when he came to see me. He didn't kiss me or sleep with me at night. He would just come in and sit and talk. He told me how what Nico did wasn't because of anything Madeline would have done to provoke him. Nico escalated quickly when things went bad and would often lose control like that. This time Madeline was in his line of sight and she didn't stand a chance.

Sometimes he would just come in and ask if I had questions, or bring me my meals, but otherwise that was it. I never understood until the day I watched the recordings why Ares had distanced himself from me. We ran hot and heavy at first, and it shocked me when he pulled away. But now, knowing that he was the one who was going to show me the recordings, it made sense to me why he did what he did. Most people would think I was crazy to stay. But where would I go? I had considered reaching out to Mario. Trying to get to him, but then realized my heart would shatter if I walked away from them.

I had only been here for a couple of weeks, but I had fallen madly in love with each one of them for their own reasons. I knew they didn't love me yet, but I hadn't lost hope that maybe someday they would. Our lives were a complicated disaster from the day we were born. This world wasn't glamorous. No one would admit the Mafia was still alive and well in New York City. But they happily call Dante Corsetti their Don. It was time for me to move forward or move on. I need to speak with each of them. Lay out some ground rules and determine what the future was going to look like. I wanted them to take me to the estate to see what they left of it, and I wanted a meeting with my cousin. The biggest thing I wanted for the world to know that I had not died the night that they destroyed the Romanos.

I opened the door to my room and found the hallway quiet and empty. The house, in general, seemed to be calmer this week. Not as much staff, not as many guards. It made me wonder if Dante had called off the troops just to give us some space. I also knew that none of them really left to do anything important. Ares told me that Nico was spending time in the woods. Not sure what that meant. And that Dante wouldn't stop working and wasn't sleeping, which wasn't surprising at all. I went to him first.

I knocked on the door that I knew was his bedroom. It was one of the few rooms in the house I hadn't spent time in other than the first night when I was searching for Nico. I spent so many nights with Ares it made me question why he had never invited me into his space.

"Yeah, I'm coming."

The door opened and there he stood. His long hair was wet and falling on his shoulders. His chest was bare, covered, and the most beautiful tattoos I had ever seen. He had a towel tied his waist and was otherwise naked. My mouth dropped open at the sight of him, and I suddenly forgot every reason I had made my way to his room. I wanted to taste him. I wanted to devour him. I wanted to —

"Valentina, did you need something?"

"I um.... yes I. I wanted to talk to you. I would like to talk to all of you."

"Together or...?"

"Um. Yeah, probably together would be best."

"Just let me dressed. Do you wanna meet in the office or somewhere else? Is everything okay?"

I took a step back. I needed distance. His body was distracting, and I needed to focus on the task at hand.

"How about the library? I like it in there and we don't use it near enough. Can you ask the others to meet us there?"

"Yeah, sure. No problem, I, um... I might need to go out and see if I can find Nico though."

"Is he not here?"

"No, he's on the property. He's just... It's okay, don't worry about it. I'll go get him. Just give me a little time. I'll send Dante to see you."

"Yeah. Okay."

I turned around and made my way towards the main part of the house. Since I hadn't left my room in a week, it felt strange being back. I made my way down a long corridor and across the courtyard into a small building that was attached to the main house. There was just a sitting room there and a small library that I had grown to love. I had never seen any of the guys in it and wondered where it came from or whose it was originally. The books inside were everything from classics to erotic romance stories. I loved all of it. I took a seat on an overstuffed chair that was in the corner. As much as my body wanted to touch them all, feel them all. Be with them again. I needed some distance in order to gather my thoughts.

I wasn't waiting long when Dante opened the door and came in.

"I heard you'd like to speak with us all."

"I would. If that's okay with each of you."

Dante didn't sit down, but wandered around running his long fingers over the old books in the library. Pulling on some and pushing them back in. He was mesmerizing to watch. It didn't matter what he did, I was always drawn to the man.

"You know this library belonged to my grandmother. I remember as a child, when my grandfather built it for her. Those were back in the days where the men of my family valued the women they had. It was for their fiftieth wedding anniversary that he had this building built for her. He had it filled with all the classics and then she went and filled it with all her smut," he laughed, "It was a constant argument between the two of them. He would always play as if it bothered him. She would read fantasies of other men. But he did it with a smile. Unfortunately, she only had a chance to enjoy it for a few years. When she was diagnosed with cancer, I thought the man would never make it through. I was young, but I could hear him up at night crying. There's something very strange about listening to a man you held in such high regard fall apart over a woman. Her death changed something in our family. My grandfather died of a broken heart only a year later and my father took over. He and my mother were together for a few years. Long enough to conceive me, and then she realized how horrible he could be. My mother died when I was born, or at least that's what my father told me. I learned as I got older that was a very common lie in our family. I always wondered if it was something else. If he had…. If he had something to do with her death. There's a difference between a toxic love and a toxic relationship. Toxic relationship is one that will destroy you and that's what they had. I'm thankful every day that I got to experience the love between my grandparents. That was true love."

He turned and looked over at me. I noticed his stubble on his chin. The dark circles under his eyes. The responsibilities that fell on Dante's shoulders were vast, but he never looked as bothered by it all as he did in that moment.

"Are you leaving us, little girl? I know I should wait to ask, but it could take hours before Ares finds Nico, and I need to know now. Are you calling us together to tell us you're leaving?"

"No, Dante, I'm calling you together to tell you I'm staying."

It didn't take hours, but it took a while before Ares walked in with Nico behind him. I was shocked at the sight of the man. He had stumbled in the door as if it was impossible to even walk straight. Dante's stubble was nothing compared to Nico's. His eyes were bloodshot and his hands were muddy, as if he had been crawling around in the dirt when Ares found him.

"Nico. Go clean yourself up." Dante's voice caught my attention.

"I already tried. He wouldn't listen to me and other than turning a hose on him. I didn't know what else to do."

Dante shook his head and walked to him. Nico was holding the wall up more than himself, and I watched as Dante took his large hand and cupped Nico's face.

"Fratello, it will be okay. She's not leaving. You need to go and pull yourself together."

My heart broke at the exchange. Knowing the pain that I had caused them. If I had just dealt with everything in a timely manner, I could have avoided so much pain between us all. I stood and walked to the men that held my entire heart in their hands. Ares and Dante had blocked my way, and I couldn't reach Nico.

"Please. Let me."

They exchanged glances, and eventually Ares took a step aside. Dante didn't move. He stayed close, too close, but it was understandable. Nico was on the verge of breaking down. Maybe he already had and I didn't know it. The anger and rage that always simmered just under his skin seemed lost. Because he seemed lost. I reached up for his face with both of my hands and leaned forward, placing a soft kiss on his lips.

"I won't leave you. You said you'd never leave me. And I could never do that to you. I will always be here."

He didn't say anything, he just stared at me and then he leaned forward and placed his forehead on mine. I smelled the liquor on his breath and the lingering scent of smoke hovered around him, but I didn't care. I lifted my hands and reached around him, pulling his body tight to mine. When his arms came around me, I felt the tension break.

"I'm so sorry. I'm so sorry I made you doubt me," I whispered over and over again.

When I stepped back, I looked up at Ares, reaching for his face as well.

"I'm sorry I made you all doubt me. I told you I was here to stay, and I was. I am. I've said it before, but I knew what I was getting into and I'm not ignorant. You're right. I am smart, I am strong and I am resilient. I will move past this. We all will. But I won't continue to build our relationships with lies. You claim you want me to be one of you yet you don't keep me in the loop. It took you weeks to tell me what had happened. All that time I sat around thinking my family was missing me, my friends were wondering where I was, and the entire time they were all mourning my death. If this is going to work and we are all going to move on, then it has to stop. Lies of omission are lies too, and I won't stand for it."

Ares was first to speak. Dante seemed to struggle with the idea of full disclosure, which I had expected he would.

"Okay, I will agree with that. Lying to you nearly killed me and it's the reason I wouldn't be alone with you, which hurt even more."

"For this to work, you all have to agree."

"Ragazzina, there are things that happen sometimes and they have not been confirmed. So those aren't things that we discuss regularly. They wouldn't be things you would need to know or things that would affect you."

"Everything you do affects me. Whether you believe that or not, I'm not going to budge on this."

"Fine. You will take your spot in our family, stand by our side and learn our business."

I looked over at Nico, who still couldn't look me in the eye. I reached forward as he did to me so many times and grasped his chin, lifting his eyeline to mine.

"I need your agreement."

"I agree," he grunted.

"I also will not spend my life in hiding. People need to know that I'm alive. I am the heir of the Romano's estate and I also would like a meeting with my cousin Mario."

"No, absolutely not."

"Dante, this is not up for discussion. I don't know what he's trying to do right now, but I will not risk any of you. He can be a greedy asshole and he's only ever been motivated by money."

"I thought you two were close?" Ares asked.

"We were as children and, to be honest, he's the only person I even spoke to now. But hearing what you had shared with me, I'm not surprised. He's young and ignorant. I won't allow him to run around with my family name and pretend that they entitle him to anything."

"Romano is not your family name anymore. You are a Corsetti now."

"I will always be a Romano by blood, but you are right. I am in Corsetti now. It is the name I planned to have at the age of eighteen and the name I plan to die with."

"Fine. I will set up a meeting with him. But the three of us will be there as well."

"No, he'll never talk with you all there. I need to find out what he's really after, what he's trying to do. I need to assess the risks to our family, and I can't do that with you over my shoulder. You will need to trust me with this."

Dante broke away from where the four of us were standing and paced the small library that we were in. I knew this would be difficult for him. I wasn't even certain he trusted me enough to allow me this chance. But I also knew in order for me to find out what was really going on, what Mario was really trying to do, that I needed to meet with him alone.

"You can come with me, but wait outside the door. Drive me there if it helps, whatever makes you comfortable, but Dante, I need to do this. You know that I do."

"No, you don't. Ares can find out what we need. Can't you?" He turned to Ares.

"Sure, in time, I always can, but I need time and we don't have the right people yet. Mario is pulling people to him that don't work for other families. He's crossing lines with gangs in the city and many of them have come to me asking who he is and what he could possibly want with them."

"They've come to you?"

"Yes, my little doll. I'm often the man on the street, for lack of a better way to explain it. You said to me the other night you don't know who I am or what I do. I do a lot of things. The businesses that I run, like my tattoo shop and the biker bar, are where I gain most of the information we need. I have men that work for us in every aspect of this city, from Wall Street to the gangs in the least affluent areas. I know how to get the information I need when I need it. But your cousin Mario is not following any normal patterns. He isn't doing what we expect of him, so we need to be cautious."

"I know he'll tell me."

"We'll travel to the city tonight and stay at the penthouse for a few days. I'll figure out a way to make this work for you, Ragazzina."

"Not tonight." I looked over at Nico. "Let's wait until morning. We all need some rest."

CHAPTER NINETEEN

VALENTINA

We had been in the city for a few days. The penthouse here was the exact opposite of the villa. It was bright and modern and sleek. I didn't hate it, but it didn't feel like home. I missed the estate and wanted this part of everything over with. Nico was dragging himself back together while Ares was working around the clock to uncover what he could about my cousin. Mario's parents had both died when he was a child. He was five years younger than I was and came to live at my father's estate. He never really followed the rules, so when Ares told me he was not following the typical patterns, they would see for someone who's attempting to rise in power, it did not surprise me. What did surprise me was how quickly he accepted a meeting with Dante, not knowing what it would be for.

Mario wasn't exactly the type of man who would gain an audience with the Don of New York City, but here he was receiving a phone call and being requested to show up at the club tonight. My men owned an upscale social club in the city. It was normally was crowded with men in suits and the women they hired to entertain them for the night. I only knew about it because Mario had taken me here once when we were younger. I remember getting drinks at the bar and giggling over the fact that I wasn't twenty-one yet and he was going on and on about how someday he would be like the men that owned this place. He always admired men who were callous and rude and wanted to be one of the men who ran one of the families in the city. Most of the families would have representation here every night, but tonight the club would be closed for a private event. Our event.

Ares had sent out word the Kings would be in town and the club would be closed for them and their own audience. He hand-selected who would be there and their guests. I learned that when the three of them planned for a night out, they wanted to know who they would be with and avoid any interactions with those they did not want there.

I was getting dressed in more clothes Ares had provided for me. Luckily, the man had good taste because the closet here was full as well.

"You look gorgeous." Dante's voice made me jump and smudge my mascara I was trying to put on.

"You scared me, and now I've made a mess," I complained as he came up behind me and turned me to kiss him.

"Oh, I've seen you much messier than that little girl."

"How is Nico?"

"He's okay, I think he'll be alright tonight. He's a bit on edge with everything that you have planned, but he's coming back to us."

I wiped the mess I made on my face while Dante watched me in the mirror. "Is this common? Does he lose himself often?"

"No, not that often; it's not as common as it once was. Nico has his demons and sometimes they win."

"I'm the reason it happened this time, and I'll never forgive myself for that. He's barely speaking to me, even now."

"You can't take any blame. Nico is his own man and makes his own decisions. Just like we all are."

I nodded and stepped forward into his embrace.

"Are you almost ready??"

I stepped back. "Yes. I am. Let me grab my purse and we can go."

"Your cousin will arrive around eleven. That gives us about an hour to ourselves. There will be a lot of people there who will have questions for you."

"I know."

"And do you remember everything you will say?"

"Of course."

"Then we should get on our way."

Our driver took us around the back of the building and through a private entrance. Then up an elevator to the top floor of a very large skyscraper. One that I knew belonged to the men I was with. I looked around and realized I'd never get used to the amount of money they had. The elevator emptied into a hallway. And I felt Ares' hand at my back as he turned us into what appeared to be an office. There was a woman sitting there behind a desk.

"Gina. I'd like you to meet. Valentino Romano."

"Romano? It's a pleasure to meet you."

"You as well."

"Is it her? She's finally here."

"Yes, she is."

"Well, it's about time." Gina smiled at me and then ran over and hugged both Dante, Ares and, lastly, Nico. "I am so happy for you all."

"We have a meeting with Mario Romano, her cousin, at eleven. I expect that he'll be taken from the front and brought to one of the meeting rooms. I don't want him mingling with the crowd, I don't want him out of sight. He will meet Valentina and he will leave. Do you understand?"

"Absolutely. Ares sent me a picture of him earlier today. Our men will take care of it."

"Very good. Now we have a few people that we need to meet."

Ares and Dante changed places, and Dante held my hand and placed his other hand on my back as we stepped out into the club. It was a warm summer night and too muggy for my liking, but the short black dress and high heeled strappy sandals that I chose from Ares' collection would be enough to keep me cool. Heads turned as soon as the four of us stepped out of the hallway that the office was in and into the club. People stared and leaned in, whispering to each other. I didn't know if it was for my benefit or the fact that all three of The Dark Kings were standing there in front of them. My men seemed to have an effect on people that others did not.

Dante directed me over to a private booth that was roped off. He gestured for the waitress, and I sat down with Ares and Nico on either side of me. After he told the waitress what he wanted for the night, a line formed and people were waiting to speak with him. The red velvet ropes kept them all just far enough away from us. But I still felt as if I was a monkey on display at a circus.

"Mr. Corsetti, it's good to see you. Please meet Michael Albert. He's in town for a while and will work with me for the time he's here. We appreciate the opportunity you've offered us both and wanted to stop and give our thanks."

"Good to meet you, Michael." I watched as the men left and two others came up.

"Don Corsetti. It's been a long time. Remember me? Do you? From the old country? I knew your father and when you were a boy. Your cousin Micah still handles all my finances."

"Yes. Of course. It's good to see you again. How are your son and daughter?"

I sat there, astounded by the amount of people who approached Dante and Ares offering well wishes and thanks for all sorts of jobs that they had or did. I learned more in that one hour, observing them here, than I had in a lifetime of studying who they were and the weeks I'd spent living under their roof. Nico seemed pleased with the fact that nobody approached him. I reached for his arm and looked at the time on his watch. I was still without a phone, so I had no idea if we were getting close to the time I needed to meet my cousin. Sure enough, we were. It was ten minutes to eleven.

"I'd like to use the restroom before meeting with him. Can you show me where it is?"

"Anything for you, la mia bella ragazza."

Nico took my hand, and Dante and Ares both looked back at us. Ares stepped aside from the people who he was meeting with and leaned into my ear.

"It's not time yet."

"No, but I'm gonna use the restroom. Nico will come with me. I'll be fine."

Ares exchanged a look with Nico and then nodded. If I had believed in psychic powers, then I would believe there was definitely a link among these three men. Ares and Nico moved around Dante, as if they had expected anything that he ever needed. It was weird how in public they rarely spoke but they just would exchange a look and move on. I suppose that's what happens when you grow up with the same people that you get into business with. Never in my life had anyone been that close with me, so I always found it interesting.

The club had gotten busier than it was when we had first gotten there. Even though everything was closed for a private event tonight, it was still packed with people. Too many people, and it was making me uncomfortable. These people kept staring, and they were probably wondering how the hell Valentina Romano was standing in the middle of the Social, a club owned by the Dark Kings, when she was supposed to be dead. I stayed close to Nico and leaned in as we came to a stop in front of the bathroom door.

"I don't like the way people look at me."

"I can make them stop."

"No, I just... I wonder if it's because I'm supposed to be dead, or if it's because I'm with all of you," I said with a nervous laugh.

"It doesn't matter. Either way, if they make you uncomfortable. I will make them stop."

I shook my head and gave him a soft kiss on his cheek. I knew Nico would threaten anyone who looked at me strangely. And threatening would be the easy way out for them. He'd just as easily kill for me. He was my monster in disguise. My tortured soul that needed healing and he was all mine. I stepped away from him and our arms stretched between us until my fingers broke away from his. I opened the door to the bathroom and let out a small gasp. If a public bathroom in a nightclub could be gorgeous, then this was it. I stepped into one of the private rooms and locked the door behind me. As I sat there taking care of business, I listened as three very loud, laughing, drunk women made their way into the bathroom. I rolled my eyes at the comments they were making over the hot, tattooed, brooding man standing at the door. That was my brooding man they were talking about, and if they kept it up, I would have something to say about it.

"I think I saw him with a woman," one of the girls said.

"Yes, someone said it was a Romano, the daughter of that old guy that died."

"The one that burned up?"

"That's the story. You never know with those kinds of men."

I held my breath, trying to listen to their every word. They were talking about my father. They were talking about me.

"People say The Dark Kings killed him and now it's more obvious than ever. How else would they have gotten their hands on Romano's only daughter?"

"That guy outside is one of The Dark Kings?"

"Yeah. That's Nico Marchesi. The crazy one."

"Everyone says Dante is ruthless, which I'm sure he is, but Nico the executioner and Ares, the model-looking one, are just as crazy. Maybe even more."

"So, what are you saying? They burned her house down and took her for themselves?"

"That's the rumor. Well. That's one of the rumors."

"Could you imagine? And she stayed with them? What a crazy bitch."

"Or a lucky bitch. They may be nuts, but I'd take anyone of them for myself."

I had had about enough. I washed my hands and stepped outside to find three rather shocked drunk bitches who looked like they had just seen a ghost.

"You know I was brought up in this world, and I learned very early on not to believe everything I hear. I was also taught not to talk shit when I don't know the people around me. You should probably learn that, too."

"I'm sorry I... I didn't know you were in here."

"Right. Because if you had, you wouldn't have been talking shit about me while you were washing your hands and painting on another layer of makeup. One more thing. The ruthless Don Corsetti, Nico the executioner and Ares the model are no longer on the market. They are all mine, not just one, all of them."

I walked past them, opened the door, and stepped into Nico's arms. That was just the motivation I needed to prepare myself to meet with Mario. Fucking assholes who thought that they deserved more than what they had were the bane of my existence. Just like the bitches in the bathroom talking shit about me and how crazy I was to be with my men, Mario would learn soon that he didn't stand a chance coming between us either.

"Everything okay?"

"Yep. All good. Time for a family reunion."

"Let's stop by and tell Dante and Ares that I'm taking you. They'll wonder why we didn't come back."

People just parted like the Red Sea when we walked back to our seating area. No one wanted to get too close to Nico, or maybe no one wanted to get too close to me. Either way, it worked to our advantage. In no time, we were back in front of Dante and Ares. Dante leaned forward and pulled me to him, kissing me. His tongue tangled with mine and my body leaned into his. That he could ignite that fire within me, and so quickly, was always shocking. Nico hadn't let go of my hand, so it appeared we were putting on a show. Dante let me go and stepped back as Ares stepped in. He whispered into my ear. Telling me all the wonderful things he planned to do once he finally got me to himself. I was beyond ready. Ares holding himself back from me was the worst kind of foreplay. Tonight would be the night. Tonight, I would finally have him. He kissed me softly, and I felt Nico pull me in the opposite direction.

"I won't be long."

Both of the men nodded to me and then turned back to the others who were talking to them. It only made sense that Nico was the one to come with me. Even though they all wanted in the room, I knew that would never happen. Mario would only talk to me. I believed that in the deepest part of my soul. And I needed to find out what his plans were. We took the elevator down a floor and walked through a marbled hallway with brass lights that hung to keep it lit. Nico opened the second door on the right and sitting inside was my cousin, Mario.

"There is a God above." He stood, running to me in some weird show of excitement. "Oh, my beautiful cousin. You're alive and well. I knew it. I never believed that they had taken you... I mean that the fire had taken. You must be so upset over your father. He was a good man. My condolences to you."

I let him hug me and place a kiss on my cheek, but that was the extent of it. I looked back at Nico. "I'll be fine. I'll be out in a minute."

I could tell by the look on his face he didn't like it, but he pulled the door closed behind him. Mario didn't seem to have anyone with him either, so it was just the two of us. Ironic, really.

"Where have you been, my dear cousin? Why have you been hiding? Are you in danger?"

"I suppose I should ask you that, am I in danger?"

"How would I know?"

"Well, as you mentioned, I've not been around. I have essentially been in hiding and you've been out here in the world picking up the pieces since my father's death. Haven't you?"

"I tried to do what I could in order to keep everything afloat. I'm not sure if you heard, but your father's business partner, Angelo Costa, the one you would have married, was arrested recently. Him and quite a few families that were involved in his business were all taken in so it's been a bit of a setback for the Romano estate."

"You are talking about the trafficking? How him and my father used to sell young girls to old men?"

"I um… I didn't realize you knew about that."

"There are a lot of things I know, Mario, and I learn more every day. So, what are your plans now?"

"My plans. Um. They haven't really changed. I still have the restaurant and will continue to run it. But if you need my help to rebuild, then I am here for you. Have you decided what you want, Valentina? Now that your life has changed so much."

"I've made some decisions, yes, but there are still a lot of things up in the air."

"Like what?"

"The Dark Kings have helped keep me safe and I owe them a debt for that. I'll need to repay them."

"We had hired men of theirs to find you. Have you been with them the whole time?"

"You hired men, Mario? With what money?"

"Angelo and I, we had worked together when your father had passed to find you. He was heartbroken. He was looking forward to the wedding and I suppose you're still betrothed, are you not?"

"No. I would never marry Angelo Costa. And to be honest, Mario, I'm surprised that you believed I would."

"I mean, I know he was older than you, of course, but your father had said that—"

"My father is dead, and no one decides for me anymore but myself."

"I see."

I watched as Mario shifted uncomfortably in his chair. He had a nervous twitch and continued looking down at his phone, then up at the door.

"Are you expecting someone?"

"No. Why would you ask?"

"Because you can't keep your eyes off the door."

"It's nothing. Tell me how you've been over the last few weeks. I can't imagine what you went through running from the house. How did you find your way to the Kings?"

"As you know, it's not like I have a driver's license or even an ID, so I did what any crazed woman in need would do. I ran to the nearest gas station and called this club."

"This club?"

"Yes, I remembered it from when you took me here. When I heard the shots, I knew I needed to get to people who would help. Gina answered that night and she runs the club. She sent Ares to get me and they brought me back to their house. I've been staying as a guest ever since."

"Why didn't you go to the police?"

"I think you know the answer to that question, don't you?"

"Right."

"Are you still staying with them, or have you been to one of your father's properties?"

"You know it's funny. When someone dies, you can't just waltz on to their property and claim it as your own. You also can't just walk into a bank and ask questions trying to gain access to funds. Lots of red tape."

Mario was sweating now. I could see the small beads above his lip and at his temples.

"I guess I didn't realize it would be that hard for you. Can I... is there anything I can do?"

"Funny you should ask—"

Suddenly, the door slammed open and when I turned, I saw the last man I ever would have expected to see was standing there. The distraction he caused was just enough for my cousin to gain an edge. I hadn't even heard him stand. I hadn't felt his hands on me until it was too late. The needle pierced my skin and my body felt heavy and weak. I looked up at the person responsible for this. The one standing over me with a wicked smile on his face and opened my mouth to tell him to fuck off, but found my eyesight was dimming, and before I knew it everything went dark.

CHAPTER TWENTY

DANTE

Ares' phone rang for the third time in a row. This time, he finally reached for it and answered. I watched out of the corner of my eye as he spoke. A look of horror came over his face and he reached for my arm. My heart raced and I knew in my gut it was Valentina. Something was wrong. He pulled the phone away from his ear and looked at me.

"They are coming for her. Now."

We took off running toward the stairwell. My mind tried to reconcile what we knew. They couldn't get her, not here. Nico was with her. He'd die before he let someone get to our girl. I pushed past Ares and opened the door to the floor we had set the meeting up on. I had Gina set up a conference room, nothing special but something private enough that the two of them could speak. Now I was kicking myself in the ass for setting up something so far from where we would all be.

I pushed open the door that led to the hallway and came to a dead stop when I saw my brother in a heap on the floor. Ares kept running and reached down to feel for his pulse. I couldn't move. I was frozen. I knew before he had even confirmed it. Nico was fine, but Valentina was gone. Ares stood and reached for the door. He opened it and stumbled backwards, leaning against the wall.

"Fuck!" he shouted and turned to punch the wall, cracking the drywall in the process.

I couldn't breathe. I leaned over, placing my hands on my knees and gasped for air. How the fuck did this happen? In my own club, in my own building, right under my nose, they got her. Mario fucking Romano was going to die for his role in this. I didn't give a shit what she thought about it either. I'd put the bullet through his forehead myself, or better yet, I'd let Nico loose on him.

Nico. Fuck. I grabbed my phone and called down to the men we had brought with us.

"Shut down the building and send four guys up to the meeting rooms. Someone is going to need to transport Nico."

Ares was holding his hand at a weird angle, which probably meant it was broken. "And call Dr. Anders. Have him meet us at the penthouse."

"For Nico? He'll want to know what happened," Leo asked.

"No, for Ares. Maybe Nico too."

"He'll want to know what he's stepping into."

"Broken bones, and I think Nico's knocked out. Maybe drugged."

"Is Valentina with you?"

"No, they got her, and no one leaves this building until you find out every person who's involved."

"Yes, sir."

I left Ares standing with Nico and made my way back up to the club. Like a madman on a mission, I ran into Gina's office.

"She's gone."

"Who?"

"Valentina. They took her."

"How the hell did they get in here?"

"I don't fucking know. Pull the goddamn cameras while I deal with the assholes out in the club."

I didn't stand behind to wait. She knew how much Valentina meant to us and probably felt as guilty as we did that this happened here. The first fucking night we took her out of the house and this is what we get. I swear I would burn down this entire city down if I don't find her. They may have thought Nico was the crazy one, but they hadn't seen anything I'm capable of when a loved one is taken from me. I walked out to the main part of the club and headed straight for the deejay. He shut everything down without question and I grabbed the microphone.

"There has been an incident and I'm afraid to tell you until my staff gets to the bottom of it, you are all here to stay."

There were some shouts from idiots thinking this was a good thing, but most people were exchanging glances nervously at one another.

"Valentina Romano was just taken from here against her will. We know who has her. Now I want to know which one of you turned on us and helped it happen."

I handed the mic back to the deejay as a crew of my men descended on the club, pulling people aside one by one and questioning them all. I looked out over the crowd to see Gina waving me down.

"What is it?"

"The video. Come here, you have to see this."

Ares stepped out of the elevator, still holding his hand to his chest as I was about to walk into the office.

"Where's Nico? He came to a couple minutes ago, but he's not fit for the public eye at the moment."

I shook my head. This wasn't the time to lose our shit. I needed his head clear.

"It took all four men you sent up to restrain him. He's a mess, man. I don't know how much use he will be to us right now."

"Fuck."

I walked into the office and leaned over the monitor.

"Here, I stopped it right as they entered the hallway. You'll never believe who's with them."

Gina was right, the second I saw her make her way down the hallway and towards Nico I knew Valentina never stood a chance. As far as we knew, she was dead. Nico had insisted that was the case. But there she was, healthy as a fucking horse, walking towards him. It made sense it was her. She was the only person who could get close enough to hurt him. She didn't waste any time. either, as soon as she got close enough, she leaned in to hug him and his body dropped like a bag of bricks.

"I thought she was dead?" Gina asked.

"We all did." Ares said as we watched a team of five men in suits make their way down the hallway and into the conference room. Four men led by the devil himself. The only one stupid enough to lay claim on our girl.

Envy: A Dark Captive Mafia Romance

When the needle pierced her skin Valentina's mind went straight to her tortured soul. All three of her men would be furious but Nico would be broken.
Check out what happens next by starting Envy: A Dark Captive Mafia Romance

About the Author

USA Today Best Selling Romance Author Nikki Rome has been a romance junky since a young age. As a girl she reached for book after book, looking for that happily ever after she always believed in. She loves all forms of romance and you can find her latest read not far from her reach. Nikki writes contemporary romance with a touch of danger and kink. Her love of realistic characters who face real problems provides a story that touches the hearts of many. As a writer, reader and lover of words, it only made sense that she publish her stories.

Now years letter she owns and manages Smut Lovers: The Community. A group of like minded individuals that come together to talk about their love of all things smut.

You can find her hosting Smut Lovers: The Podcast or running Smut Lovers: The Conference. Either way you know she'll always be talking about her love of books.

www.NikkiRome.com

Facebook

TikTok

Made in the USA
Columbia, SC
19 May 2024